PRAISE FOR
TEMPLE ALLEY SUMMER

★ "This imaginative tale, enchantingly written and charmingly illustrated by veteran Japanese creators for young people, has a timeless feel. . . . An instant classic filled with supernatural intrigue and real-world friendship."

— *KIRKUS REVIEWS*, Starred Review

"A sweet ghost story, a mystery, an eerie and unsettling story-within-a-story: Finally, the work of the great Sachiko Kashiwaba, one of Japan's most revered children's authors, is available in English translation! I'm so pleased that young people who read in English can now enjoy Kashiwaba's *Temple Alley Summer*, and experience the pleasure and wonder of viewing the world from a less familiar angle." — LINDA SUE PARK, Newbery Medalist and *New York Times* best-selling author

"A charming, suspenseful tale that grabbed my imagination and kept me turning the pages to the very end!"

— CATHY HIRANO, translator for Hans Christian Andersen Award–winner Nahoko Uehashi

"What a thrilling discovery this book is. There are unexplained legends, ghosts, and plenty of twists and turns to keep those pages flying, but at its heart it's a story about a sensitive boy who wants to do the right thing, even when things get strange and his ordinary life is suddenly filled with the most unsettling mysteries. It's a story about friendship and about believing, and a thoroughly captivating read."

— DANIEL HAHN, award-winning translator and author, founder of the TA First Translation Prize

"Utterly enchanting! Part mystery, part ghost story, this magical tale has the makings of a classic."

— SUZANNE KAMATA, author of *Pop Flies, Robo-Pets, and Other Disasters*

"As a kid, I would have loved reading this compelling story within a story grounded in a Japanese boy's school and home life as he protects a girl ghost. I love it now!"

— ANNIE DONWERTH-CHIKAMATSU, award-winning author of *Beyond Me* and *Somewhere Among*

"Fans of Hayao Miyazaki will love *Temple Alley Summer*. . . . This beguiling tale — skillfully translated and charmingly illustrated — imparts haunting, hopeful lessons about second chances and what it means to fully embrace life."

— **LEZA LOWITZ, author of *Up from the Sea***

"In this absorbing, multi-layered story, the past, the present and an unfinished fairy tale are all satisfyingly connected. . . . This bewitching book makes me hope more of Sachiko Kashiwaba's works will be translated into English."

— **SUZANNE MORGAN, Politics and Prose (Washington, DC)**

"This middle-grade novel exemplifies the joys of reading children's books in translation: experiencing cultures other than one's own. Kids familiar with Japanese culture from Studio Ghibli films, though, will feel right at home in this contemporary ghost story!" — **ROBIN STERN, Books Inc. (Campbell, CA)**

"*Temple Alley Summer* is like a three-in-one book — a manga-like feel, a modern Japanese story, and fable, all in one. I loved the ghost girl, Akari, and the genuine Kazu. . . . One of my SUMMER PICKS!!!" — **KIRA WIZNER, Merritt Bookstore (Millbrook, NY)**

"A tenderly written and thoughtfully translated book about family, friendship, grief and new beginnings which made me laugh and cry — sometimes at the same time."

— **DENISE TAN, Closetful of Books (Singapore)**

"In this engrossing translation by Avery Fischer Udagawa, Sachiko Kashiwaba's *Temple Alley Summer* delivers a page-turner of a mystery, a paean to the transformative power of stories, and one intrepid fifth-grader's quest to discover how those we have lost might return . . . and whether they should!"

— **PHILIP NEL, Director, Program in Children's Literature, Kansas State University**

"Middle grade readers (and beyond) will love this thrilling and heartfelt book."

— **MELEK ORTABASI, Chair, Department of World Languages and Literatures, Simon Fraser University**

"In *Temple Alley Summer*, Sachiko Kashiwaba spins an intricate yarn that celebrates the power of story to overcome even the greatest obstacles. . . . A story for anyone who has ever lost themselves in a good book and will do anything to learn how it ends!"

— **JENNIFER MACDONALD WHITMAN and NATHANIEL FORREST WHITMAN, co-authors with Margaret Read MacDonald of *Teaching with Story: Classroom Connections to Storytelling***

TEMPLE ALLEY SUMMER

Sachiko Kashiwaba

Illustrations by Miho Satake

Translated from the Japanese
by Avery Fischer Udagawa

Restless Books
for Young Readers

BROOKLYN, NEW YORK

Copyright © 2011 Sachiko Kashiwaba
Illustrations copyright © 2011 by Miho Satake
Translation copyright © 2021 Avery Fischer Udagawa

First published as *Kimyōji Yokochō no Natsu* in 2011 by Kodansha Ltd., Tokyo. Publication rights for this English edition arranged through Kodansha Ltd., Tokyo.

First Restless Books hardcover edition July 2021

Hardcover ISBN: 9781632063038
Library of Congress Control Number: 2021933874

Restless Books gratefully acknowledges the support from The Japan Foundation for this publication.

 **JAPAN**FOUNDATION 国際交流基金

This book is made possible by the New York State Council on the Arts with the support of Governor Andrew M. Cuomo and the New York State Legislature.

NEW YORK STATE OF OPPORTUNITY. | **Council on the Arts**

Cover design by adam b. bohannon and Sarah Schneider
Text design by Sarah Schneider
Cover illustration by Miho Satake

Printed in the United States of America
1 3 5 7 9 10 8 6 4 2

Restless Books, Inc.
232 3rd Street, Suite A101
Brooklyn, NY 11215

www.restlessbooks.org
publisher@restlessbooks.org

TABLE OF CONTENTS

TEMPLE
ALLEY
SUMMER

CHAPTER ONE

A Ghost at My House!

I never dreamed my house had a secret unknown to my parents or me—and believe me, when I discovered it, I had no plans to get involved. I am a scaredy-cat.

The whole thing began because I frighten easily, or because it was summer. Or maybe because my grandpa died this past spring.

I shouldn't have learned the secret at all. But from the morning of the day we had multigrade activity time at school, or really the day before, I was involved.

It was a sticky, hot July night. The TV ghost story shows, typical for summer in Japan, came on at seven. A scaredy-cat like me had no business watching them, I know. But I couldn't *not* watch, either. I had to see: *Dishes rattle in a hotel late at night, though no earthquake registers. A ghost with long hair keeps pace with a car doing forty miles per hour. A hand appears forming a "V" over the middle person's head whenever three people have their photo taken at a certain scenic spot.* Could it happen? I was hooked. For three hours. It was a ghost story marathon.

"Kazu, you'd better quit it," my older sister nagged at me. I glared back at her. She meant that I should quit both watching TV and eating the watermelon I was snacking on. To be honest, I was thinking I should knock off the watermelon myself, but then she said it:

"Don't come crying to me in the middle of the night asking me to take you to the bathroom."

She shot me an icy glance.

My sister's in seventh grade and I'm in fifth, and since last spring our two bedrooms have been next door to each other. I would never go running to her bedroom at night. Ha! I grabbed a fifth slice of bladder-loading watermelon to prove it.

I should have known better.

My eyes shot open. I had to pee and fast. I looked at the clock: not yet four a.m. The sky was pitch black, the same as at midnight. I wanted to cry.

My house is old, built by my grandpa when he was young. We live in it while my parents renovate a little at a time. The place is pretty big.

To reach the bathroom from my room on the second floor, you have to go down a flight of squeaky steps, past the storage room, past my grandpa's old bedroom, and next to a room with tatami floors that faces a porch and has the family altar inside. The add-on bathroom juts into our grassy courtyard.

Since there's no way to reach the bathroom quickly from upstairs, anyone with stomach trouble sleeps on the floor of the tatami room, close to the toilet.

My mom keeps saying we'll renovate the house to make it spacious and modern, but until we have the money, this is just a pipe dream.

Anyway, it was a long way to the bathroom, and scary, so there was no way I could go. I had no plans to wake my sister and have her take me either, thank you very much. I knew how she would react. But I had to pee. *Help!*

Time for emergency measures. I opened the window. A light rain was falling—perfect. If I peed on the roof from the open window, the rain would wash away the evidence.

It was hardly the first time I'd done this. I pee out the window every once in a while. Especially in winter, when I get so cold going down to the bathroom that it's impossible to fall back asleep. My window opens onto the courtyard, so nobody sees me, but there *was* the time last winter when Mom saw evidence of my pee in the snow on the roof.

"We still have your ducky potty from when you were a baby!" she said, glowering. *Um,* I will not use the ducky potty! I told Mom I would never pee out the window again, and she calmed down. Now I just avoid getting caught.

This time, everything went smoothly. My pee made a sound, but it was masked by the rain, so there was no chance of my parents hearing anything as they slept downstairs.

Joro joro . . . as the pee left me, the tension drained from every part of my body. I exhaled so deeply I almost sighed out loud.

Then I heard a noise below.

CRASH.

My body tensed up again, but there was no stopping the pee.

I squinted toward the sound and saw the sliding door near our altar room slip open. No one was outside. Was a thief about to escape? Or a family member sneaking out of the house? My Uncle Junichi who lives with us often goes out fishing or hiking. But Junichi's been in China since last year, with his former university professor, helping out with an archaeological dig. I knew it couldn't be him.

My pee stopped, and I felt a bit better. Just then, through an opening in the faded curtains behind the sliding door, I saw a pale foot. A child's foot. My sister's? Not possible since she was asleep in her bedroom. I would have heard her if she'd used the stairs. And her feet are tanned, not pale—she swims on the swim team, so her legs are darker than mine.

Then I saw a figure step from behind the curtains. Wearing a kimono. A white one. Even the sash was white. The child had shoulder-length hair that was pulled back on one side. The sky had brightened a bit, so I could see two small, bright red baubles on a hair band. The baubles were the size of pickled plums and perfectly round. Because the child was looking down, the face was hidden.

Who was it? A child robber? The hands were empty. And the kimono was exactly like the one they put on Grandpa when he died. Thin and snow white.

A ghost, whoa! A ghost! It had to be.

I forgot that I had just seen the feet. People say that real ghosts have no feet, but is it true? I only thought about that later.

"G-ghost! A ghost!"

I wanted to scream, but my voice got stuck.

Still, the figure stepping into the courtyard sensed me. I saw thick, pitch-black hair swing around and a face tilt in my direction. I think I saw the face, but I didn't meet the eyes.

This time I screamed for real.

"GYAAA!"

As if pushed by an invisible arm from the foot-wide windowsill where I stood, I fell back and landed on my bottom.

"Ghost! Ghost! Ghost!" I shouted.

For the first time ever, I lost all strength in my body. All I could do was sit and stare at the window.

The impact of me falling on my butt made our old house shake.

Mom, Dad, and my sister came running to my room.

What followed was torture.

We discovered that a lock on one of our sliding doors was open, and the wooden gate that leads from the court-yard to the alley was ajar. "We probably just left them open, though," my mom said.

No one believed I had seen a ghost.

"You idiot, I told you not to watch those shows," my sister said as she conked me on the head with a fist and headed to her room.

"You agreed to do your business in the toilet, young man." Mom seemed ready to chew me out for the fore-seeable future.

"It's only four. We can still get some rest," my dad offered. "Kazu, are you OK? Can you get back to sleep by yourself? Do you want me to stay?"

My only ally.

I told my parents that I'd fall asleep on my own, but my mind was racing. *I saw what I saw. I saw!* For a long time after that, I lay awake.

When Mom shook me later that morning, it was past eight. I had slept soundly, without dreaming. This must be what they call the sleep of the dead.

"Kazu! Get up! We're late. Even I overslept because of you."

Mom flew out of my room as soon as she saw me struggle to sit up.

"I'm out of here!" my sister yelled from the front door.

"Shake a leg, it's after eight!" Mom barked at Dad as she ran downstairs.

"Stop shouting, I'm up," Dad grumbled from the bathroom.

Everyone was late and crabby, even Dad. There was no time for breakfast. I grabbed a slice of bread and ran out the door.

The light rain of early morning had become a downpour.

~~~

Third and fourth periods of school that day were multigrade activity time, our last of the spring term.

My school, Uchimaru Elementary School, sits in a shopping district with centuries of history. Most of the kids' grandparents, not to mention their parents, went to the same school. People have kept up a neighborhood association that runs traditional events year-round.

Multigrade activity time means that kids from grades one to six break into their neighborhood association groups instead of their grades. Younger students spend time with upperclassmen, learning how to succeed at school and developing respect. That seems to be the point of it, as far as I can tell. Mostly we do recreation, like dodgeball or demon tag, and the little kids behave okay. We do pretty well if we just listen to the sixth-grade leaders. The sixth grade at my school has four girls who are born leaders, and the fifth-grade class has several ready to take their place. That leaves me on easy street. Other kids complain that my group has too few older students, but I don't mind multigrade activity time.

Today, though, we had to stay indoors because of the rain. The school gym was closed for repainting, so no recreation. We stuffed ourselves into a conference room to look up old names for the sights in our area.

Who gets these ideas? My money is on the vice principal, nickname: Broad Bean, who is obsessed with local history.

Of the seventeen kids in my group—the Minami Ōdori Shopping District group—sixteen stood huddled around a map that lay open on a desk. (I sat to the side, stifling a yawn.)

"Wow, a map from 1913. I can't believe they have this."

"Must be a copy."

"The regional castle used to be here. Whoa, in 1913 the grounds were already a park."

"The Naka River is here. Naka River Bridge is over here too. Same place as now, right?"

"The park is there, so yeah."

"So Minami Ōdori must be here."

"It has a different name, doesn't it?"

"'Ōmi district, Gofuku area.'"

"Here's a blurb: '*Ōmi district.* Established near the castle by Ōmi merchants during the feudal period, when each regional lord traveled between his domain and Edo, which is now Tokyo. The goods of Ōmi merchants were highly favored in the capital. Ōmi district included numerous clothing and ocean product stores. Kimono sellers, or *gofukuya*, later separated and formed *Gofuku area*. Traditional footwear, accessory, and handbag stores also flourished in this bustling area.'"

I could hear the students murmuring, prompted by the leader, as they examined points on the map. I myself sat slumped at another desk, picking my nose. If you can avoid getting caught by a teacher, a relaxed posture is the way to go.

"Hey, there's no Park Heights!"

"Duh, it's an old map, it wouldn't have English names."

The kids leaning over the map kept bumping heads with each other. One head had some red baubles on it. They looked exactly like the ones I'd seen on the ghost at my house that morning. *You can buy those baubles anywhere,* I told myself. Yet I kept glancing at them without meaning to.

"Yūsuke, isn't this your family's store?"

Someone pointed to the map.

Yūsuke is my best friend. His family has run a kimono and clothing store for generations. He went to look.

"You're right," I heard him say.

Yūsuke turned around then, his eyes scanning the room. For me.

"Hey Kazu. Kazuhiro. I found the street where your family lives," he said.

He pointed to the map like the kid before him had done.

"Hmm, really?"

I stayed in my chair and nodded instead of standing. I wasn't exactly fascinated by my family's street being on the map. Unlike Yūsuke's family, we're not generations-long shop owners. We're a bunch of regular worker types.

"It says your street is called Kimyō Temple Alley!" Yūsuke added.

"What?!"

Two or three people reacted at the same time. As if that were a signal, they all laughed.

I thought I had misheard. Kimyō Temple Alley? I had never heard of Kimyō Temple.

Some of the students in the group turned to look at me. I finally stood up.

"What'd you say it's called?"

"Kimyō Temple Alley."

Yūsuke beckoned me with one hand.

As I approached the map, the other students parted like the Red Sea for Moses. And I saw those red baubles again.

The area Yūsuke showed me was labeled Kimyōji Yokochō, or Kimyō Temple Alley. It was written in formal ideographs with tiny phonetic marks to help people read it.

"Is it really the same place?" I said, scanning the map.

I found the area labeled Ōmi, which seemed to be the former name for Minami Ōdori. At its center was the store called Takamatsuya, Yūsuke's store. The place really had been around for generations—it was on an antique map! Ten stores east of it was a street—my street—connecting Minami Ōdori to the Daiku area, which runs parallel. Same as today. The street is about a hundred yards long with four or five houses on each side. And its name? Kimyō Temple Alley. At least on the old map.

"Kimyō Temple? I don't know about any temple," I said with a scowl.

"Does the map show one?" A sixth-grade leader took a look. There were no temples even close to my street.

"The temple district is way over there."

"The map is from 1913, right? Maybe there was a temple before the map was made."

"Maybe there was a graveyard too! Scary!"

"Live there, and you could get hexed!"

"I saw that happen on a TV show!"

"I saw that too!"

The conversation turned from Kimyō Temple to the TV specials the night before.

Fine for you guys, I thought. *No hexes at your house. What about me? I live in the back alley of a haunted temple.* I scowled some more.

"Let's finish up, people," a leader directed.

The students sat down and opened their notebooks.

I opened mine, too, for what it was worth. No way was my house on top of a graveyard. Or was it? Maybe that was why I'd seen the ghost.

Then I saw the red baubles across from me and off to one side. The head beneath them looked just like the one I had seen before dawn. There was no mistaking that outdated hairstyle. The girl with the baubles faced our leader, who had begun to speak.

She's the one. The one I saw. The ghost who left my house before dawn!

"Ah—!"

Before I knew it, sounds were escaping my mouth as I stood up, knocking over my chair.

"Kazu, what's up with you?" Yūsuke said, staring at me.

"That person, she's a ghost. A ghost!" I sputtered, eyeing the girl as she looked up at me, wondering what was happening. Everyone else did the same. They had no clue who I was talking about.

"Why? Why is she here?" I murmured.

Yūsuke tugged at my pants. "Sit down, Kazu. Sit *down.*"

When I finally heard him, he pointed across the room with his jaw. Vice Principal Broad Bean was glaring at me.

I sat.

~~~~

That girl is the ghost I saw at my house. What's she doing here?

I stared at the red-baubled head. The girl wrote briskly in her notebook as though nothing had happened.

"Kazu, what's the matter with you?" Yūsuke spoke in a low voice so as not to be heard by Broad Bean.

"Why is that person here?" I asked him.

"Who do you mean?"

"The girl between that second grader, Tomohisa, and Yamada's little sister."

"Akari Shinobu?" Yūsuke asked like it was no big deal.

I was shocked. "You know her?"

Yūsuke frowned and poked me. He thought I was playing.

"It's Akari, dude. Akari," he repeated.

"That's her name?"

"Kazu, what's wrong with you? Akari's in your class!"

"She is?" For a second I was speechless. No way could she be in my class. I would know her if she were. "She can't be."

"Come on, Kazu, Grade 5, Section 1. Are you OK? Quit joking."

Yūsuke made his scariest face, as if to say my joke was not funny. Tell me about it. Nothing funny at all.

"Did you hit your head? You've been out of it since this morning."

Now Yūsuke peered at me closely, looking worried. I couldn't say anything else.

"Her name's Akari," he continued. "You've known her since kindergarten—no, before kindergarten."

He waved a hand in front of my eyes. I wanted to say that he was the crazy one, but I stopped myself.

The girl that Yūsuke had called Akari was writing something in the second grader Tomohisa's notes, helping him out. Tomohisa nodded politely. Tomohisa is the kind of kid who gets nervous around strangers. He would never talk to someone he had just met, much less let that person to touch his notes. When he came here as a first grader last year, we all had a hard time getting him to hold hands for games, even with classmates, let alone the older students. It took six months to get him to do that, and even longer to get him to say hello and smile.

So Tomohisa was like Yūsuke. He also knew Akari Shinobu.

Did that mean Yūsuke was correct, and I was nuts?

But I knew. She was definitely the ghost who had left my house that morning. It was her face I saw. Her eyes I nearly met. Akari seemed to sense that I was watching her and glanced up. When she met my gaze, her expression changed as if to say, *What?* Quickly, I looked away.

"Does she live in my neighborhood?" I asked Yūsuke. I was supposed to have known her since before kindergarten, after all.

"Do you seriously not know? Is this a game?" Yūsuke thought I had made up some bizarre rules and begun to play a game all by myself. I do this sometimes, so I couldn't blame him for asking. "She lives closer to you than me," Yūsuke said. "Right there in Kimyō Temple Alley."

He used the name we had just learned.

I felt totally lost. I still had no memory of Akari.

~~~~

When multigrade activity time ended, I returned to my classroom. So did Akari.

I'm in small group four in our class section, and Akari is in group one. Her group's five desks were pushed together to make a kind of table for lunchtime. Last I knew, that group had only four desks that formed a square at lunch.

We ate our meal of fried sweet buns, cucumber salad, white fish, and frozen pineapple.

"How many kids are in our class?" I asked Ami Yamagata, who was eating her fried sweet bun next to me.

"Thirty-three," she answered.

The number had gone up by one! I thought we only had thirty-two.

"Our teacher is Jirō Harukawa, nickname: Country Music. The hamsters we're raising are Boneless and Moochie. Our class leaders are Yōichi Sakura and Mizuki Yamabe. Is that right?" I asked.

Ami chewed her food, looking exactly like Moochie the hamster. She nodded yes.

Akari was the single detail I could not remember. I knew everything else.

Ami stared at me like Yūsuke had a moment before, then added, "And you are Kazuhiro Sada. An Aries. Blood type O. Grade 5, Section 1 pet coordinator. Nickname: Third."

Yes, that's me. In the youth sports program I was part of until recently, I covered third base in baseball. When my teacher Country Music heard that, he said, "Kazu, you seem to be third in a lot of things, don't you?" Everyone agreed: in terms of smarts, sports, and even with girls, I always come in third.

"It's because you don't let other people see the real you," my sister told me. "You're not straight with them. That's what keeps you from rising to the top."

What's so bad about being third? I want to know. I like not sticking out. I enjoy doing my own thing, my own way, in someone else's shadow. I still got chocolates from two girls on Valentine's Day this year. That may have been only a fifth of Yūsuke's take, or less—he's heir to a kimono dynasty, after all—but getting chocolate from two girls is no joke. One of the girls was Ami, but anyway.

"Kazu-kun, are you OK?" Ami asked. "You sound like my grandma."

"Your grandma?"

"She asks really basic questions sometimes. They're worried it's dementia."

Dementia. She might as well have punched me in the head. I started to panic. I wondered if you could get dementia at my age.

"Sorry to hear that. Never mind what I said."

I wished I could swallow my panic with my lunch, but that was impossible.

Akari's red baubles bobbed down the road ahead of us as Yūsuke and I walked home.

The rain had stopped after lunch, but the temperature outside had skyrocketed. I could see steam rising from the wet surfaces.

"I have to go to cram school now," Yūsuke complained. "Tomorrow too."

Tomorrow was the last day of school before summer. Our closing assembly would finish in the morning, but Yūsuke still had to study afterward because of his cram school teacher's schedule.

"See you tomorrow then," I said, parting ways with Yūsuke in front of his house.

Tomorrow night was also the start of the summer festival at the local temple dedicated to the goddess Kannon. We go there every July the evening after school ends. It's a big deal for Yūsuke and me—and every grade schooler in Minami Ōdori—because for us, the festival means summer vacation. It's ingrained in our brains.

After I said goodbye to Yūsuke, Akari's red baubles began to take over my mind. I watched as she turned onto my street. Kimyō Temple Alley.

"Yūsuke was right." I couldn't believe it. She really lived right by me.

Our neighbor, Mrs. Uesugi, came walking from the other direction. Akari, who wore a pink vinyl backpack, said hello to her.

"Akari-chan! How have you been? Almost summer vacation, isn't it?" Mrs. Uesugi replied.

So she knew Akari as well. I really was the only one who didn't know her. In shock, I stopped walking.

"Kazu-kun, you're back!" I heard Mrs. Uesugi call to me and quickly nodded.

Akari turned into the side road between Mrs. Uesugi's house and an apartment building called Miyoshi Cottage. As if on a leash, I followed her.

Akari walked up to a house directly behind Mrs. Uesugi's. A shrub with orange blossoms grew next to the small front gate. The nameplate on the gate read SHINOBU.

She lived so close to my house—practically on top of it. Had her house been there all along? If not, what had? I felt like the house should be there, and then again maybe not. I couldn't remember for sure. The house was common enough, cream-colored, two stories, with a gray roof. The cherry tomato plant in the yard had fruit hanging from its branches.

"I'm home," Akari called from the front door.

I watched from the front gate with my eyes wide open.

The door swung out.

"You're home! You must be hot," a woman's voice answered.

The door opened to make room for Akari, but *no one was standing there.* Really! I didn't see anyone who could have spoken.

Whoever had opened the door was invisible.

First a ghost. Now an invisible person. What next?!

I felt helpless, like something huge had happened or would soon, and I had no idea what. All I could do was stand there with my eyes glued to Akari's house.

CHAPTER TWO

Am I the Only
Clueless One?

Akari walked into the house. The front door closed.

My feet took me around the side of the house.

I saw a small porch with a roof and a long horizontal pole for hanging laundry. The door to the porch opened.

"Even if I hang it out this late, it'll dry in a snap in this hot weather!"

A laundry hanger appeared—one of those pink plastic umbrella skeletons with clips for underwear and socks.

The hanger moved, but no one was holding it. The umbrella skeleton just floated back and forth with the dangling laundry.

I couldn't believe it. Akari's invisible mom was hanging the pink hanger from the horizontal pole on the porch. That had to be what was happening. That's how it looked.

"Say, Akari, the summer festival starts tomorrow night, doesn't it?" Invisible Mama said, directing her voice toward the house.

A gust of wind blew some white lace curtains away from the porch window. Now I could see inside.

The house was bare.

It looked as if it had just been built, or the family had just moved in—but there were no boxes like you'd see after a move. There was nothing. No table, chairs, or TV. Not even a calendar on the wall.

I could also see Akari sitting on the floor in front of the kitchen counter, hugging her knees. "Yes, the festival starts tomorrow," she said. "Um, Mom?"

She looked up.

Her voice sounded happy, but she wasn't smiling. She looked anxious.

"Worried about your *yukata*?" Invisible Mama asked as she hung a towel over the laundry pole. "I've got it all ready."

The wind blew the curtains open again as if to tell me, look closely!

"Thanks, Mom! I'm so excited!" Akari said. But she still looked anxious, like she wondered if she'd said the right thing. What was the matter with her?

Just then I heard the voice of the caretaker at Miyoshi Cottage apartments, which are next door to Mrs. Uesugi's. The caretaker has short white hair and walked along with a towel draped around his neck, using it to mop sweat from his face.

"Today's a scorcher, isn't it?"

I thought he was talking to me, since Akari was crouching inside.

But then Invisible Mama answered.

"Sure is. I thought the rain might cool things off, but it just keeps getting hotter and hotter." She sighed, and then added, "Are you off to prepare for the festival?"

"Yes, Ma'am. We do a little every day to get ready in time. We'll set the tents up today."

The caretaker raised his hand in farewell.

"That's a big job. Take care!" Invisible Mama answered.

The caretaker looked back as she called to him. He spotted me.

"Kazu-kun, hello there! Did you come to see Akari?"

The caretaker had seen Akari's mother perfectly well. I felt like someone had knocked the wind out of me.

"Who, me? No," I mumbled, and then fled.

Nothing made any sense. I was different from everybody: the only one out of the loop. The only one who didn't know Akari. The only one who couldn't see her mother. How had this happened, and why? I had no idea.

I practically dove back into my own house.

"At least say 'I'm home,' would you!"

My mom came out of the kitchen looking cross.

I'd planned on asking for help: *Mom, I'm the only one who doesn't remember Akari. The only one who can't see her mother. What do I do?*

"Mom," I began.

She took a tray with some tea and *manjū* and sat down by the TV. The rebroadcast of her favorite suspense drama was starting.

"Mom," I said again.

"Oh, Kazu, there's ice cream in the freezer. Or do you want one of these?"

She held out a manjū. She was still watching the screen.

I was beginning to lose confidence that I could explain my predicament. How could I get her to see that there was something wrong with me—and only me? Telling her might just make her worry.

I got some ice cream and sat down beside her.

"Have you seen that house over behind Mrs. Uesugi's, the one with the orange flowers blooming? It—"

"Akari-chan's place?" Mom answered before I could say another word.

Even my mom said Akari's name with a straight face.

I wanted to vanish with my ice cream. How could something this weird happen? Was my brain just messed up?

"Why are you talking like you've never seen her house before?" my mom asked. "You used to go there and play all the time when you were younger. Maybe you're seeing Akari with new eyes.

"By the way, that flowering plant is called Chinese trumpet vine. Pretty, isn't it? I wanted to plant one in our yard, too, but your grandma wouldn't allow it. Said that those are flowers you only see at temples."

Mom grumbled while still watching TV.

I remembered the other thing on my mind.

"Did you know our street used to be called Kimyō Temple Alley?" I asked.

Mom shook her head. "It's been Minami Ōdori Lane 3 since I married your father."

"Was there ever a temple here?"

Maybe the house was built on a graveyard and I was going crazy because of some vengeful spirit.

"No, I don't think there was a temple. Kimyō Temple, that's an odd name, isn't it?"

"You write 'come back' and then 'life,'" I said, explaining the characters.

"'Come back to life,' really? Sounds like zombies!"

Mom giggled, even though the thought was creepy.

Sitting opposite her, I felt my skin crawl.

Suddenly I knew. When Akari stepped out of our house, she'd worn a white kimono. She had come back from the dead. She had to be the ghost of someone who had passed away. I had witnessed her return. I didn't know why everyone else seemed to know her already, or what was happening with Invisible Mama. But Akari was a spirit who had found her way back to the world of the living through my house. She had returned to life. The fact that I alone didn't know her had to be linked to Kimyō Temple. It had to. There was just one problem: My house is no temple. My dad and his dad had regular office jobs; they weren't priests.

"Would Dad know if there was a temple here once?"

"Not sure. Why don't you ask him?" Mom answered absently.

~~~~~

It took forever for my dad to come home that day. He got in after nine, when I had just finished bathing, and his face was red from drinking. I thought his work must have run long, but he said he'd gone to a gathering of volunteers preparing for the summer festival. Like I said, our district's been around a long time. Ties between neighbors go back far, so it's hard to shirk these obligations.

"Did you know our street used to be called Kimyō Temple Alley?" I asked him.

Dad paused a moment, then shook his head. "No, I didn't. Why do you ask? Is this your summer homework or something?"

Mom perked up and leaned forward.

"Say! That's a good idea. Those summer projects where you grow tomatoes and keep journals with pictures of shoots and wilted stems must drive even your teacher crazy. How about doing your project on the history of neighborhood names this year? Interview people who know the old names! How does that sound? Dad could help you find neighbors who remember the old days."

This was no request; it was a command. Dad's face grew serious.

"Let's see, people who might remember the old names. If your grandpa were here, he would know . . . guess we need someone else his age. Mr. Suzuki next door is a good ten years younger and only moved here when he bought his place, so he wouldn't be of help. Other people I can think of have already moved away. Families who've been on this street for years . . . we might be the only ones."

Dad frowned at the discolored ceiling, then remembered.

"Wait! Ms. Minakami might know something. She's the aunt of Ms. Satō, who lives kitty-corner from us. I remember about twenty years ago, when the first apartments were built, she said owning a house was a pain and passed hers to Ms. Satō. Then she moved into the newly built Minami Heights."

Dad clapped his hands together.

"Right, that was just about twenty years ago. Ms. Minakami is about two years older than your grandpa. She decided to get an apartment sometime in her sixties." He nodded as memories of his younger years came flooding back.

"Well, apartment living is certainly easier: no snow to shovel, only one lock to check, and no grass to mow—unlike here," Mom pointed out.

"Yes, dear, I'll mow on Sunday," Dad replied. "But with Ms. Minakami it was more about being trendy, I think. That's why she moved."

Dad added that Ms. Minakami was a flashy dresser.

"Let's see, if she was two years older than Grandpa, would she be eighty-two now?" Mom asked.

"That's right," Dad answered. "I saw her not too long ago. She came to City Hall to complain about the garbage."

Did I mention my dad works at City Hall? So did my grandpa.

Dad said that Ms. Minakami was a character and used to keep her light on till all hours when she lived close by. He thumbed through the phone book and called her.

Next thing I knew, I was scheduled to meet Ms. Minakami the next afternoon at one to discuss my summer project, theme: The History of Neighborhood Names.

"Isn't this great, Kazu? Summer homework will be a breeze this year!" Mom said, looking pleased.

Mom's usually the one who really does the work on my summer project, so I understood her enthusiasm. But I wished we had stuck with tomatoes.

The closing assembly at school the next day was long, hot, and tedious, like always. When it finished, everyone looked bored and restless. Only Akari sparkled. She looked completely unlike the anxious girl who had sat in a house with nothing inside it the day before. I almost wanted to tease her and ask what was so fascinating about the principal's speech on how we should all work to avoid traffic accidents.

But when I left school later, all I could think about was summer vacation. I was one hundred percent thrilled.

I strapped on my art set, sketch board, gym bag, and indoor shoe bag and headed home with Yūsuke.

"Have you decided on your summer project yet?" I asked him.

I wanted him to collaborate with me on my project. It would be much easier to go and interview people with him along. I also wanted to talk to him about Akari. But Yūsuke had only one thing on his mind: lunch.

"Why worry about our summer projects right now? I'm starving! Hey, everyone at my place is busy today. I get to buy lunch at the convenience store."

Yūsuke grinned in bliss.

At Yūsuke's kimono store, where the staff and his grand-parents work, it's common to see his mom or his grandma boil two sinks' worth of noodles at a time, or cook curry in a pot three times the size of ours. They've served me meals lots of times. But today they had their hands full with a yukata promotion for the Kannon summer festival. So, for a change, Yūsuke was allowed to buy his own lunch. As for me, a store-bought lunch is neither rare nor exciting.

"Should I get some instant fried noodles?" Yūsuke asked me. "I haven't had those for ages! Man, my stomach is growling!"

Yūsuke started to list all the TV commercials he'd seen for convenience store food.

Meanwhile, Akari was walking along right in front of us, her red baubles bobbing up and down. There was no way I could ask Yūsuke about her now.

"Come over to my place after you eat lunch," I said. I would just have to talk to him at home.

"Didn't I tell you I have cram school today?"

I saw Yūsuke's face turn gloomy. Oh yeah, he had told me that the day before.

"I'll come after," he promised. "Might be four or four thirty. Then we can go to the festival."

Yūsuke walked off, muttering that they would probably serve fried noodles at the festival, so he would buy some-thing else for lunch.

~~~~

I wound up wolfing down some of Mom's famous grilled rice balls and going to meet Ms. Sato Minakami at one all by myself.

Ms. Minakami lived in Minami Heights apartment 902 and said she was eighty-two, no, eighty-three years old. But her back was ramrod straight and she stood a good four inches taller than me. Neither thin nor fat, she seemed the picture of health.

Her apartment had a pink, white, and gold striped sofa and frilly curtains, Western style. The iced tea she served in fancy glasses on her marble table clashed with the *senbei* rice crackers she arranged in a basket.

I opened my notebook so I would look the part.

Ms. Minakami's hair was dyed brown and set in a trendier style than my mother's. She had pale skin, bright red lipstick, and hardly any wrinkles. Her mascara made her look large-eyed and, well, cute. She wore a lace-trimmed summer dress that actually tied in the back with a ribbon. I would laugh if my mom wore that, but it didn't look too bad on Ms. Minakami. She even smoked. She was a character, that was for sure, but as I sat facing her, I saw that everything about her sort of fit together.

"So you're Gen-chan's grandson?" she said. "That was too bad about Gen-chan. I went to the funeral, you know. This past March, wasn't it? It was cold. My circle of acquaintances keeps shrinking and shrinking these days . . . but I get to make new young friends just like you. Living a long life is worth it!"

Ms. Minakami flashed a grin.

Gen-chan was my grandpa; his name was Genji Sada.

Ms. Minakami crunched her hard senbei loudly. It looked like she would live for a while yet.

"I wonder why they called that street Kimyō Temple Alley?" she said, not saying whether she knew the answer. She looked at me as if trying to make out why I wanted to know.

"It seems strange, since there's no temple close by," I replied.

"True, it does seem odd. So that's how you came up with your project?"

Ms. Minakami looked at me curiously. I got a bad feeling. If she didn't know how the street got its name, I wished she would just say so and be done with it.

"It's kind of creepy, isn't it?" she said. "*Kimyōji*, 'return-to-life' temple. It makes me think of those people in movies, um . . ."

She waved her right hand as though reaching for the word.

I supplied the word my mom had used. "Zombies."

"Zombies! Right." Ms. Minakami nodded. "Zombies are scary. Have you seen one?"

Suddenly, the look in her eyes was scarier than any walking dead.

"The ones in movies are obvious zombies," she went on. "They've got those ripped-up clothes and big, dark circles under their eyes. You can almost smell that they're dead. But there are other zombies who look exactly like you and me. Zombies who look like regular people."

I was surprised. "There are?"

We seemed to be drifting off topic.

"Sure! Some zombies live right alongside ordinary people," Ms. Minakami said. "They've got some nerve. To think a dead person could live next door to you, eating ramen like it's normal. How awful!"

Ms. Minakami shivered.

I wanted to tell her she could say what she liked, but zombies are not real. Thinking about them made me feel funny.

"Have you seen one?" she asked again.

I swallowed. "Have I seen a zombie?"

She nodded, looking serious.

She had totally forgotten my school project. I hadn't come here to talk about horror movies. I sighed softly.

"They go around just like you and me," Ms. Minakami went on. "But there are people who can spot them. People who know the undead when they see them. What did you call them again? Zombies. There are people who can see through that ghost skin of theirs!"

Ms. Minakami raised her face suddenly, acting dramatic.

She seemed to be saying that I could see through the skin of ghosts. And suddenly I started to make a connection. But what did Ms. Minakami want from me?

As if reading my thoughts, she narrowed her eyes.

"Have you seen one, Kazu? There are people who see them the moment they come back to the world. Is that what's happened?"

Her voice was light, but her eyes were intense.

It hit me that she was asking about Akari. I did not say yes. I held back. There was no way I would admit such a big secret to Ms. Minakami. I didn't like her. I had just figured that out.

"Where do they come back from?" I asked casually. I even tilted my head.

Zombies, dead people, ghosts—all of them come back to life in temples, according to legend or something. But my house was no temple.

"Well, my boy, good question. They must come back from heaven, right? That's how it was in a movie I saw long ago."

Ms. Minakami dodged my question. I knew it was a dodge. I felt confused. I frowned in frustration, but I still got nothing out of her.

"I'm sorry, Kazu. You came all this way but I couldn't help you. Wait a minute, though. Your question is about a temple, so maybe someone at a temple could help you!"

Ms. Minakami clapped her hands together. She was acting dramatic again, but I ignored that.

"Hmm," I said, nodding vaguely. "I'll give that a try."

Before I could say anything else, Ms. Minakami had taken out her cell phone.

"This is Sato Minakami. Thank you for the other day . . . Yes, yes. No, today I'm here with a young man who wants to know about Kimyōji. I couldn't help him. He's Mr. Sada's grandson. Yes, Mr. Sada."

Ms. Minakami sneaked glances at me as she talked. When she finished, she collapsed her flip phone with one hand.

"You're in luck. The priest at Ryūseiji says he can talk to you. Do you know how to get to the temple district? It's easy enough to get there from here."

Ms. Minakami told me to wait a moment, while she wrote the telephone number of Ryūseiji and drew a basic map on a piece of paper.

"Will the priest at Ryūseiji know about Kimyōji?" I asked.

"They're both temples. He'll certainly know more than I do."

Ms. Minakami pushed the paper at me.

"Uh, thanks."

I felt that what she was doing was less a kindness than an interference, but I accepted the paper. I had no choice, because she even folded my fingers around it.

I unfolded the paper and looked at it. Temple district. I sighed. The temple district was three or four bus stops from Ms. Minakami's house. Too close to pay the fare, so I'd have to walk. In this heat. And at two, the hottest time of day, I would melt on the asphalt.

"Why don't you take a taxi?" Ms. Minakami offered, as if reading my mind.

She forcefully opened a white chest of drawers trimmed with gold and took out her wallet. Some glass figurines and framed pictures on top of the chest rattled. She seemed determined to get me to this temple.

"No, thank you. I can get there on foot."

I knew better than to accept her money. I could already hear my mom scolding me for taking cash from someone I barely knew.

I jumped to my feet.

I headed down Ms. Minakami's front hallway and felt relief as I stepped into my sneakers by her front door. Her apartment was cramped. I wondered how many rooms it had. Ms. Minakami lived alone, but there were families of four living in places the same size as hers. I liked my house, I realized, even if I had to walk miles to the toilet.

I learned then that Ms. Minakami did not live alone. As if to announce my mistake, a cat yowled.

"Nyaaa!"

I turned around to see a black cat the size of a small dog. Ms. Minakami picked it up with effort.

That was her cat? I'd seen it before. It walked around our neighborhood like it owned the place. Like it was the local cat boss.

"Kiriko, this is Kazuhiro-kun. He's going to Ryūseiji now."

Kiriko. She had pretty impressive whiskers for a lady cat. I said nothing.

She yowled a second time, showing me the red insides of her mouth. I felt scolded for not responding.

Kiriko glared at me with her blue eyes. I said goodbye— to Kiriko or to Ms. Minakami, I wasn't sure—and made a beeline for the elevator.

I walked through the Minami Heights lobby to the drive outside and finally felt better. Ms. Minakami was one strange old lady. Most people mellow as they get older, but her edges had sharpened with time. I looked back at the ninth floor. It was the top floor. Idiot mistake.

Ms. Minakami was leaning way over her balcony railing, watching me. I felt her eyes bore into me.

"Go to Ryūseiji!" she ordered with a wave.

Her voice reached me all the way down on the ground. Without thinking, I nodded.

I sighed as I trudged through Minami Ōdori. It was hot. It would take me less than twenty minutes to walk to the temple, but the whole thing was starting to seem like a chore. I didn't have to go right away. I didn't want to go alone. I could go later with Yūsuke.

My feet turned toward my house in Kimyō Temple Alley.

"NYAA!"

Kiriko. The cat sat at the entrance to my street, blocking my way. When had she run past me? It was as if she had magically appeared and was scolding me, saying, *Hey, where do you think you're going?*

I was starting to drive myself crazy. How could I possibly know what a cat was saying? Pathetic. Even more pathetic was that I was afraid of Kiriko!

"My mistake," I said. I actually said that.

Then I made an about-face.

CHAPTER THREE

Strange Old People

headed for the temple district.

Without turning around. I knew that Kiriko was still behind me, tailing me at a distance of several yards. I could feel her blue eyes on my back.

A car pulled up beside me and stopped. It was a fancy red car, kind of a brick red but brighter, and American: flashy and huge. Yūsuke would have recited its make and model on the spot, but I just thought it was big.

A window lowered to reveal Ms. Minakami inside. She wore sunglasses.

"I remembered an errand I have to do. I'll take you to Ryūseiji, Kazu-kun," she said, and then added, "Well, Kiriko! Fancy meeting you here. You hop in, too."

I realized later that Ms. Minakami probably doubted that Kiriko's tactics would be enough to get me to Ryūseiji. At the time, though, it was hot, and I was tired of dealing with Kiriko, so I got in.

The cat and I sat beside each other on the cream leather back seat. Ms. Minakami had filled her apartment with frilly stuff, but the interior of her car was sleek. The only decoration was an amulet from a shrine in our neighborhood, which dangled from the rearview mirror. My family has one of those, too. The amulet looked odd in the American car.

"This automobile is called a Mercury. It looks like a hungry bear, doesn't it? They say that all drivers should give up their licenses at seventy, but people don't understand that the older you get, the more you rely on a car. Try waiting for a late bus in this heat for ten minutes. I would dry to a crisp!"

Ms. Minakami's big bear crept through the tadpole-like Japanese cars and got me to Ryūseiji in less than five minutes.

"Thank you," I said. When I bowed, who should appear at my feet but Kiriko.

"She seems to like you," Ms. Minakami said. "No need to worry, she's never been lost. She'll make it home. See you later."

I didn't know if she meant she'd be seeing me later, or Kiriko. *See you, Kitty, and keep a close eye on Kazu-kun!* That could have been her meaning.

After that, the bear of a car bounded off like it had spotted its prey. *Wow, it both creeps and pounces,* I thought. I'm pretty sure my jaw dropped.

"Nya—*aa!*"

Kiriko meowed at my feet as if to say, Get moving.

I couldn't ignore the animal, so I began to walk.

In obedience to Kiriko, and with her still tailing me, I headed through the entrance to Ryūseiji. Before me lay a path of white gravel without a single leaf or piece of trash on it, leading to the temple's main hall. To the side was a narrower, winding path that skirted some shrubs. I figured it led to the priest's residence.

Which way should I go? I looked back at Kiriko. She caught up and headed for the residence. I followed.

The entrance to the priest's quarters was open. Beside it, a Chinese trumpet vine was heavy with flowers. My mom said my grandma hated those flowers because you see them at temples, but I thought they were pretty.

I couldn't see anybody around, but the second I set foot inside, a priest appeared as if he'd been watching me. He wore a white vestment with what looked like a black skirt around his middle.

"You must be the young Sada boy Ms. Minakami mentioned. I've been waiting for you since she called. Come in, come in."

How old was he? He could be in his forties, like my dad. Then again, if someone told me he was over sixty, I'd believe it. It's hard to tell with a man whose head is shaved. His face was ruddy and shiny, as was his pate. No wrinkles. If it hadn't been for his clothing, he would have looked exactly like a pro wrestler—and a villainous one, at that. His voice boomed from his large chest as if strengthened by sutra chanting.

"Kiriko, you made it," he said.

The cat *was* on a mission.

I glanced at Kiriko in disgust.

"Kiriko is friends with my cat Tama," the priest told me. "Tama's under the weather these days due to the heat. You came for a get-well visit, didn't you, Kiriko? Good kitty."

The priest made a show of trying to pick up Kiriko. Just then, another cat yowled outside. Would that be Tama? Maybe the priest had told the truth. Kiriko slipped from the priest's large hands and ran off.

Unlike Kiriko, I couldn't make a clever escape. The priest had me in his clutches. And he kept calling me a young boy, which I hate.

I couldn't hide the sour look on my face, but the priest showed me into a fancy reception room, anyway, and told me to sit.

"Ms. Minakami told me about your summer project. I'm impressed. Impressed."

He had a habit of repeating the ends of his sentences. He sat at a big table as if to block my exit. The table was huge, the priest was built like a mountain, and the unreadable fancy calligraphy on a scroll in one corner was also big. I felt miniature, like a Lilliputian in *Gulliver's Travels*. Like I might disappear completely.

"I hear you're researching the old names of places in town," the priest continued. "How did you come up with such an idea? For a growing young boy like you, this subject seems dry to me. Seems dry."

The priest's wife appeared from behind him to serve cold barley tea and *mizu yōkan*.

"I heard that the street where I live used to be called Kimyō Temple Alley," I said. "We looked it up during multigrade activity time at school. It's an odd name, especially since there's no temple."

After repeating my story, I gulped my tea.

"I see. So, you learned about this at school? It's a funny name for sure. 'Come back to life' temple. Creepy too. Dead people coming back and living among us like it's no big deal. Scary. Scary."

The priest's mountain-like body shuddered. He really did seem scared.

The more I watched the priest, the more I noticed that he was acting just like Ms. Minakami—talking more about the return of dead people than Kimyō Temple itself. Something was weird. I would have understood if someone told me *why* it was bad for the dead to return—like if they dragged the living into the world of the dead or something—but neither of them had explained. They just went on and on about how creepy it was that the dead came back and lived among us.

I could tell that the priest wanted to ask me about Akari. She was the only ghost, or the only returned-to-life person, that I had seen. But I wasn't going to satisfy his curiosity. If Akari had come back from the dead, was that so wrong? Was she bothering someone, living with Invisible

Mama and looking worried? What was so scary? It was strange, and maybe a little spooky, but I didn't think it was *creepy*. Not like Ms. Minakami and this priest. I realized that I had taken Akari's side.

"Hmm, I hadn't thought about Kimyōji like that. Do you really think that people coming back to life is creepy?" I asked, playing dumb.

"You don't think so? They're ghosts. Ghosts!"

The priest dangled his hands in the air and mimicked a ghost. He was such a beefy, healthy ghost that he looked silly.

"So you think it's possible for the dead to come back?" I asked.

The priest grew uncomfortable. "Well, it's right there in the name—Kimyōji. Kimyōji."

He laughed nervously.

"So there *was* a temple by that name?"

I opened my notebook and gripped my pen.

The priest rambled for a while about the history of the temple district, but eventually said he had never heard of Kimyōji.

By the time I left Ryūseiji, it was after three.

What am I doing? I wondered, sighing aloud.

Ms. Minakami and the priest both knew about Kimyōji but were hiding it. I could tell. They were trying to cover up Kimyō Temple's story while getting information from me. They knew that I knew, or was hiding, something. And I was—Akari. Yet they hadn't really learned a thing from me, or I from them. All I knew now was that they wanted me to talk about Akari. I might still talk it over with Yūsuke, but I had no plans to confide in any more adults about her.

I thought of Akari sitting alone in her empty house. I felt sorry for her, even angry for her. I couldn't get her off my mind—even if she *was* a ghost.

Kiriko appeared behind me again, like a shadow. I had an uneasy feeling that the cat might figure out what I was hiding. I couldn't trick her like I could the showy granny or the pro wrestler priest. Despite the heat, I felt a cold sweat break out as I walked home.

"I can't believe I came all the way over here and still don't know anything about Kimyō Temple," I muttered. "I'm sick of this!"

I wanted Kiriko to hear me. It was absurd that I was paying so much attention to a cat.

She kept following me. All the way home. I thought she might even come inside my house. Yūsuke would be on his way over soon, and I wanted to talk with him about Akari. With Kiriko there, I wouldn't be able to.

I squatted so I was face-to-face with the cat and summoned my courage.

"You like me, don't you, kitty? That's fine. You can come live at my house. It's bigger than Ms. Minakami's place. Run around here for a while and you might even lose some weight. I'll warn you, though, my mom doesn't like cats much. She might have to put a leash on you. But you can take it, right? And you can handle having only rice and miso soup to eat. My mom makes the broth from real fish, not a mix."

The cat was huge with thick fur. Ms. Minakami clearly fed Kiriko like royalty. About the time I mentioned the diet of rice and soup, the cat turned and stalked off. Sweet relief. To think a cat could boss me around like a bully! It was so pathetic that I couldn't even laugh.

After I got home from Ryūseiji, Yūsuke came over when cram school ended, looking like his brain was fried. We still had some time before the festival, and I pondered how to bring up Akari as Yūsuke sat on my bedroom floor, his nose stuck in a manga book.

Just then, my mom came to get me with a scary look on her face. "Kazu, what did you do!" she hissed.

"Huh?" I had no idea what she meant.

"The head of the neighborhood association and the president of the seniors' group are here. They want to see you!"

"They do?"

"Don't 'they do' me, Mister!"

Mom motioned me downstairs.

"They came to see me?"

"They did. Now hurry up!"

Mom was in the worst mood I'd seen in days. Neither of us knew why the district elders had invaded our house.

The two old gentlemen sat formally in our tatami room. The neighborhood association head was the retired owner of Yabuya, a noodle restaurant. The president of the seniors' group was a man I had seen around town, but I didn't know which family he belonged to. He was completely bald in front. Both of the men wore pinched expressions, as if this visit were a huge bother. There was a fan oscillating in the room, but they both flapped their folding fans impatiently to cool themselves.

I wanted to sulk a bit myself.

"So, you're Kazuhiro-kun?"

The head of the neighborhood association looked at me and put on a smile.

Mom yanked my arm to make me sit. "Has my son done something of concern?" she inquired. Wearing a tight expression, she looked across the low table at the men.

"Not at all. We've learned your son is doing some research."

"The priest at Ryūseiji told us and thought we might be of use to Kazuhiro-kun."

"There was a parishioners' gathering at Ryūseiji today."

"We're impressed by your son's project."

The two men took turns talking as they sized up my mother and me.

"Ryūseiji, the temple?" Mom asked, startled. She turned to look at me.

I nodded. "I went to talk to Ms. Minakami about my summer project and she drove me to Ryūseiji to see the priest."

"So now these gentlemen are here to see us?" Mom's jaw dropped.

"You told me to do my project on historical names, remember? I started working on it and ended up going a few places today. I still don't know very much." I produced a record-breaking scowl.

"Ah—"

My mom froze briefly. Then she jumped up. "Let me bring you two some cold drinks," she said to the guests. "I apologize. You're taking precious time to help my son."

She dashed to the kitchen.

"Not to worry! We just wanted to help."

"An interest in history is something to be proud of!"

The two men called to my mother's retreating back. Then they turned to me, as if getting down to business.

"Kazuhiro-kun, what exactly do you want to know?"

I told my story again. Third time in one day. It was beginning to annoy me.

Then the men ate edamame and chilled tofu and grew flushed from the beer my mom served, and they told me how in the late 1800s the Buddhist temples and Shinto shrines were separated in Japan, and anti-Buddhist sentiment spread, and sacred images and sutra scrolls were burned. The president of the seniors' group was once a social studies teacher. As it turns out, neither man would end up telling me anything new about Kimyōji.

"I doubt such a temple existed."

"Must have been a ghost temple!"

The two men laughed at the term they'd coined.

Then they said they had to be off to the festival and struggled to their feet.

"Thank you for stopping by at this busy time," Mom said as she bowed at the front door to see them off.

As I bowed next to her, the timing of their visit struck me as odd. Today should have been a frantically hectic day for the neighborhood association, not a time to come by and offer me a history lesson. Something was up. I had a suspicion that the men had come to check on me, or to confirm something. It had to do with Akari. What I knew seemed to matter a lot to several older people in my community.

I headed for my room to talk about it with Yūsuke, but Mom stopped me. She had gone to clear the men's dishes and came hurrying back.

"Kazu, one of the guests left his folding fan. Run after him and return it, will you?"

She thrust the fan at me.

I had no choice and jogged out the front door.

The two men were just turning out of our street.

"I can't believe Ryūseiji called us about him, even though we've got the festival tonight," grumbled the head of the neighborhood association. He slumped his shoulders.

I knew from earlier that he was hard of hearing. That must be why he spoke so loudly. I could hear every word he was saying. I hid behind a telephone pole.

"But the boy doesn't know much, does he?"

"No, he's just doing his schoolwork. And the project is his mom's idea."

"True. He didn't want to go to Ryūseiji."

"What I want to know is who started this. Who blabbed about Kimyōji?" The neighborhood association head clicked his tongue.

"Did he say they studied a map at school?"

"That's right. Must've been Broad Bean's doing."

Even the old men knew my vice principal's nickname!

"Fellow fancies himself a historian."

"Nothing but trouble, that one. Didn't he come from the next town over? He doesn't know a thing about local history. He thinks he does, but he's barely scratched the surface."

The two men laughed, almost giggling, and hurried away. I decided to return the fan later.

Now I knew it for certain. There *was* a secret, and it *did* involve Kimyō Temple. Ms. Minakami, the priest at Ryūseiji, and those two men were all in on it.

"*Have you seen one?*"

I pictured Ms. Minakami's eyes when she asked me that question. What I had seen was Akari. What those adults all wanted to know about, was Akari.

When I got to my room, Yūsuke looked up from the manga.

"Did you have diarrhea or something, Kazu? You were gone for ages."

Well, at least he realized I'd left the room.

I'd hoped to talk to him about Akari, but he threw his book down.

"The festival's starting soon. Time to get going. I scored some spending money from my grandma. Fried noodles, here I come!"

He began to run down the stairs.

"Kazu, let's go!"

Well at least my attentive friend still planned to take me along. I dashed after him.

CHAPTER FOUR

A Family Secret

The local Kannon temple sat at the center of Minami Ōdori. It took Yūsuke and me less than five minutes to walk there from my house. Inside the grounds, twenty-odd vendors had set up booths, and the tantalizing smell of stir-fry sauce filled the air.

Volunteers had put up a tent that was several times larger than the temple hall itself. Inside the tent, neighborhood elders, including the two men who had visited my home, were handing out drinks to festivalgoers.

Yūsuke and I downed our stir-fried noodles first thing, and then we ate some *takoyaki*. Afterward we sat down by a wading pool where people fished for water balloon yo-yos.

A human-sized red goldfish popped up between us.

"Gotcha!" It was Ami Yamagata, dressed in her festival yukata. Four or five other girls from our class surrounded us.

"How do I look?" Ami asked.

I couldn't believe she was asking *us*.

"Perfect!" Yūsuke gave a thumbs-up as he checked out Ami's red yukata and her sash, which flared like a goldfish tail.

"And wow—Inoue, Sakko, Tanabe, Yukina, yours look great too!"

The heir to the kimono throne had a gift. He talked to the girls as if he hung out with them constantly. In return, they acted giddy and flattered. Each of them wore a yellow,

pink, or red yukata with an accessory, such as lace at the collar or artificial flowers in the sash. They looked more like exotic tropical fish than regular goldfish.

I whispered to him. "Are they all customers at your store?"

"Yes," he confirmed in a low voice. "For the past two weeks, my grandma has been holding yukata seminars and selling them all these yukata, sashes, and ornaments."

"You all look terrific!" he added loudly for good measure.

The man running the yo-yo pond narrowed his eyes in nostalgia. "Ah, the yukata are what make this the summer festival," he murmured.

"I'm so glad we took the trouble, aren't you?" Ami and the other girls fluttered, but then one of them stood up and waved.

"There's Akari!"

Akari came walking down the path that led to the temple building. She wore a white yukata with an indigo iris pattern. Compared with everyone else's yukata, hers looked more subdued and grown-up. She wore the usual red baubles in her hair and had pulled the look together with a stiff red sash.

Her large eyes widened when she saw us, and she grinned and waved. Then she looked up to one side and smiled and chatted with someone. Ah, so Invisible Mama was next to her.

"She came with her mom!" observed Yukina, waving. "We thought for sure she'd be with Misa and her friends, so we didn't invite her. We should have!"

Ami and the others nodded.

"Why'd you think she'd come with Misa?" I asked. My mind suddenly shifted to Akari again.

"Well, until last year she was in her class," Ami answered. "Don't you remember?"

Oh right, everyone else knew Akari from last year. No, wait—Yūsuke knew her from before that. Ami and the others must be the same. They not only remembered Akari from fourth grade, but they also remembered her from years ago, when we all were little. How had this happened? I looked toward Invisible Mama, whom everyone else could apparently see. Again, I saw nothing.

Then without even realizing it, I began to watch Akari as she clip-clopped along in her wooden geta.

At that moment I felt someone's gaze. One of the men who'd come to my house was watching me from the tent. He had seen me following Akari with my eyes. *Oh, no!* I panicked. I had to keep them from finding out about her—about how she was the one who had returned to life. What should I do?

Akari was saying something to Invisible Mama and looking in our direction. I raised a hand to wave. I was pretty impressed with myself, considering I had only met her the day before. As Akari waved back, looking pleased, I watched the man in the tent out of the corner of my eye. He turned away. Apparently, I had managed to act just like any nervous boy greeting a girl in his class. If the man had been Kiriko, I might not have fooled him so easily.

I wiped away cold sweat.

"Kazu-kun, do you like Akari?" Ami said next to me, poking me in the ribs. "You never paid attention to her before, but your eyes are glued to her today."

"Akari? Umm, I don't think so."

I shook my head. Ami shrugged, unconvinced.

But that was a good idea. If I acted as though I liked Akari, I might be able to fool the nosy neighbors.

As I fished for water balloon yo-yos with Yūsuke and Ami and her friends, all I could think about was why I was the only one with no memory of Akari, and why I alone could never see her mom. I kept coming back to what Ms.

Minakami had asked me, "Have you seen one?" It must be because I had seen Akari come out of my house wearing her funeral kimono. If Akari had come back to life, was my house the place where the dead returned? Was my house Kimyō Temple?

The neighborhood elders knew something I didn't. I wanted to ask someone about it, but not them. Asking Akari herself would be fastest: "Hey, are you a ghost?" But I had seen her sitting cross-legged in that empty house, looking anxious. There was no way I could ask her something so insulting. I felt bad for her. I was the only one who had seen the other side of her. I wanted to be her ally.

Wait a minute! Did that mean that I liked her, just as Ami had said?

If I couldn't ask Akari, then who else could I talk to? Should I investigate somehow? I remembered how the old men had laughed at Broad Bean, saying he was only scratching the surface—a wannabe historian. Broad Bean wasn't born here. They had mentioned that. Did *here* mean Kimyō Temple Alley? No, because the neighborhood association leader's noodle shop was not on my street. Those men must have meant that only someone born in Minami Ōdori would know about Kimyō Temple. Ms. Minakami knew about it. My grandfather, who was her age, would have known about it. If only my grandpa were alive, I could have asked him.

Then it hit me.

Akari had come back through my house. If my house was Kimyō Temple, that would be a huge deal. My grandpa would surely have told my father about something that important. Grandpa died after a severe cold turned into pneumonia, but his mind was sharp until the end. To help my father and the rest of us who would survive him, he apparently gave instructions about who would inherit our land and our house, and what would happen with money, and even who we should invite to the funeral. Would a grandpa like that have died without passing on a huge secret about our house? That was the part I didn't get.

My father had learned nothing about Kimyō Temple from Grandpa. He had told me I should ask Ms. Minakami. But—

"Uncle Junichi!" I jumped to my feet.

"Kazu, you're not leaving already, are you?"

With Yūsuke shouting crossly at my back, I took off at a run.

Uncle Junichi might have been the one my grandpa had told, instead of my father. My sister and I always call Junichi our uncle, and Junichi calls our father "older brother." He called my grandfather "Grandpa" like all of us. But my dad and Uncle Junichi are actually cousins. Uncle Junichi is the son of my grandpa's older brother. His parents passed away when he was in high school, so my grandpa raised him as his own. The reason my house is oddly large is because they connected it to Uncle Junichi's house.

I remember Uncle Junichi saying once that he felt like a freeloader, lodging at our place for nothing. But my father answered him, "Nonsense. You're head of the family."

As the son of my grandpa's elder brother, Junichi is the true heir to the Sada name.

My grandpa and the other old people put a lot of stock in things like heads of household and successors. If there were a secret in our family, my grandpa probably told Uncle Junichi, the next head of our family.

When I got home, I went straight to Uncle Junichi's room and switched on his computer. Before he left for China, he gave us his email address and said that we should email him if we needed anything, because email would be the fastest and most reliable way to get in touch.

Did Grandpa tell you anything about Kimyō Temple? I wrote to him.

His reply came sooner than I expected, at about ten that night.

Ask me how I'm doing first, would you?

I could tell he wasn't happy with my lack of manners. But his message went on. I wanted to yell, "BINGO!"

I've heard of Kimyō Temple. Apparently, there's a kind of folk religion where people pass a Buddhist statuette from one family to another. The followers might have a temple structure someplace, but they mainly make offerings to the statuette. For centuries, Japanese have worshiped at both Buddhist and Shinto altars. They seem untroubled about holding many faiths.

Anyway, a shared statuette would circulate among believers, going to a different household every year. Our street is where a number of households that shared the same statuette came together. Hence the name Kimyō

Temple Alley. During the Meiji Period (1868–1912), religions were reorganized, and the temples in our city moved to the temple district, but Kimyō Temple with its circulating statuette—and no temple building—remained as it was.

The idea with the statuette was that if you prayed to it, someone could come back from the dead. I doubt that everyone believed that, even the most devout. At any rate, during Meiji, the families in Kimyō Temple Alley began to drift away, and the statuette was supposedly burned during an anti-Buddhist movement. Other temples looked down on Kimyō Temple as a renegade congregation, which is why many details were kept private. The only people who know about it now are people from our street and Minami Ōdori—no more than a few people, your grandpa said.

Actually, the statuette that supposedly burned was hidden in our house. During the time my own grandpa was alive, they were actively still hiding it. But when my dad was alive, eventually they decided to put the statuette back on the household altar. They must have figured that no one remained who really remembered Kimyō Temple. Grandpa told me to care for it. I thought this whole story sounded a bit like the hidden Christians (the Japanese Christians who worshipped in secret in the seventeenth, eighteenth and nineteenth centuries).

Why do you want to know?

I wrote back to Uncle Junichi:
Do people really come back to life?

His reply arrived almost instantly.
I asked your grandpa the same thing. He told me it was probably just legend, but he relayed one story he had heard from elders during childhood. It must have been from the Meiji Period. These elders would have heard it from people in town. Someone had pointed at a person walking down the street and said to his companion, 'He looks exactly like your older brother.' His companion replied, 'My brother died ten years ago in the war!' But then he looked at the person and agreed, 'He really does look like my brother before he went to war. I wonder if he came back through Kimyō Temple.' The other man said, 'Perhaps your mother prayed to the statuette.' The two of them watched the mysterious person for a while, and then as they left, the man whose brother had died said, 'I'm going to tell Mom that my brother came back. She'll be so happy.' The war the brother had fought in was the Boshin War (1868-9), according to Grandpa. This was a long time ago.

Anyway, that much your grandpa had heard—and he knew that there were people who believed praying at Kimyō Temple would bring someone back to life. Because of that, our ancestors couldn't bring themselves to destroy the statuette. Instead, they took care of it. Grandpa told me I should do the same.

I wrote back:

Uncle Junichi, do you believe in it?

My uncle responded:

I believe it's natural to want people we've lost to come back to life, especially if they died unexpectedly in wars or accidents. Or even if they died after living a long, full life. I suppose it would have comforted people to pray to the Kimyō Temple statuette and then, if they saw someone who resembled the dead, they could reassure themselves that their prayer had been heard and the person had returned. It was apparently that simple: pray, and the person would return. The person who died also had to want to come back. But they would not come back to their own family; they would come back to an unrelated family.

That's the part I find a little hard to believe: you could see anyone who looked like the deceased, and the person who prayed could still think, 'Ah, he came back. What a miracle, thanks to Kimyō Temple.'

I thought about praying to have my father and mother come back, you know. Not because I had complaints about Grandpa and Grandma . . . it was just lonely to lose my folks. But if I had prayed, they would not have come back to my home. The belief was that they would come back as other people, in other families, so I decided not to go through with it.

I replied to Uncle Junichi with a question:

So, all people had to do was pray to the statuette?

~~~~

Uncle Junichi answered.

Apparently so. And according to the stories, the souls who came back looked and lived exactly like normal people. But if someone witnessed them coming back through the temple, that person would know their story. If that person kept quiet, they were fine. But if someone confronted them and said, "You are a child of Kimyō Temple," their new life would end. The whole thing seems a bit too simple to me, but anyway.

After Grandpa and me, you will be the next keeper of Kimyō Temple, Kazu. You asked what I thought, so I'll tell you: I think that if a soul comes back to life, we should let him or her live. Your grandpa said the same thing. The Sada ancestors thought so too, which is why they hid the statuette and cared for it. Grandpa told me to do the same. I told him I would. Is that what you wanted to know?

Now I wasn't sure what to do at all. Should I tell Uncle Junichi about Akari? I was feeling a little better already, just knowing that I had not gone totally crazy. That is, if I believed what Uncle Junichi's email said.

It's an unusual name for a neighborhood, so I thought I might use it for my summer project, I typed. That was all I said.

It's a family secret. You'd better not, Uncle Junichi replied.

OK, I won't. I'll grow tomatoes again, I answered. But if you remember anything else about Kimyō Temple, will you email me? G'night!

~~~

62

I wanted to go to sleep.

Hold on. Is that all you've got say to your uncle after months of silence?

After that, I had to read about all his latest news: Authentic Chinese food doesn't always taste like you expect. The food they get near the archaeological dig is average. Alas, there's no one to date. (Poor Uncle Junichi, he's past thirty but still nowhere close to finding a partner.) As I read through his message and sympathized, I had plenty to think about in a corner of my mind.

After saying goodbye to Uncle Junichi, I had the feeling there was something in his emails that I should have picked up on, but I couldn't figure out what. I reread our conversation, and finally, I hit upon what I had missed.

If my family's house was Kimyō Temple, someone from Akari's former family must have come to pray at our altar. Uncle Junichi had said it was as simple as praying to the statuette. Who could have come and prayed? After Grandpa died, a lot of people who couldn't attend the funeral stopped by to pay their respects at our altar. No one had come over in a while—but there *must* have been someone. And whoever it was must have come while I was at school.

I went into the living room, where I found Mom and Dad dozing off in front of the TV. Whenever this happens and I point out that they're sleeping, they insist that no, they're awake and watching the show. Whatever.

Mom forced herself to sit up. "Kazu, I thought you were in bed already. Summer vacation starts tomorrow. Why not get some rest?" She scrunched her eyebrows.

"Has someone prayed at our altar recently?" I asked her.

"What are you talking about? I offer fresh water and rice every morning and pray to our ancestors. Now you, on the other hand, after all you owe your grandpa and grandma—"

I was in for a sermon.

"No, no, not one of us. Someone *not* in our family, I mean," I interrupted.

"Oh, you mean have we had a guest?"

"Yes. Someone who prayed at the altar."

"Yes, actually, there was. When would that have been . . . four or five days ago, I guess. Someone who had been out of town and didn't realize your grandpa had died."

"Who was it?"

"It was a lady who lives in the Midorigaoka area. She worked with your grandpa at City Hall. Her last name was Andō, I think."

"How old was she?"

"About seventy."

Akari's mother? Or Akari's grandmother? She didn't have the same last name as Akari, but Uncle Junichi did say that the person came back to a different family.

"Where in Midorigaoka?" I wanted to know. "Do you have an address?"

"Kazu. I don't want the head of the neighborhood association coming over here again. What are you planning, exactly?"

"You were the one who told me to research old place names for summer homework!" I reminded her. "But, if you want me to grow tomatoes again, I can go and buy seedlings. I'll just need some money."

Mom complained about me doing tomatoes again, and then told me that the house was near the Midorigaoka public swimming pool. She even remembered that Mrs. Andō's first name was Katsura.

"You know where Et-chan lives," she said, mentioning a relative of ours. "When I talked with Ms. Andō, I realized she must live in the same direction as Et-chan. Block number one."

I know that area. It has some houses people built before Midorigaoka developed a new residential subdivision. Et-chan told us that the land prices were low before, so buyers could afford houses with big yards. I knew the place—I could get there easily! I decided to meet this person named Katsura Andō. I would discover her connection to Akari.

Tomorrow, I would explain everything to Yūsuke and take him with me to investigate.

On the first day of summer vacation, Mom made me wake up at six a.m. to go do "radio exercises." It's a two-minute program that airs on the radio every day.

All the old people from our neighborhood were gathered at a parking lot by the shops. A bunch of grade schoolers were there too, stifling yawns and sporting really bad bedhead. Yūsuke must have slept in. We were maybe a thirty-second walk from his house, but he didn't show up. Akari, on the other hand, had combed her hair nicely and put in the red baubles, and she looked happy. I wanted to crack a joke about how a ghost would never look that nice in the morning.

Akari and the old people exercised cheerfully. The rest of us moved like zombies. There was still no sign of Yūsuke.

I stopped on my way home and talked to Yūsuke's dad, who was cleaning up in front of the shop. "Yūsuke's in bed with a stomachache," he told me. "He ate too much at the festival last night. Did you get sick too, Kazu?" He gave me a worried look.

I shook my head. I couldn't believe that Yūsuke had let me down at a time like this. I trotted out my champion scowl.

At ten o'clock that morning, I rang the doorbell at the Andō residence in Midorigaoka.

I was proud of how resourceful I'd been. I had managed to come here without Yūsuke. I had ridden to Midorigaoka on my bike and found Et-chan's house, and as I turned the corner, I had found the Andō place.

"My name is Kazuhiro Sada. I am the grandson of Genji Sada," I introduced myself. "I hope to interview people who knew my grandfather for my summer homework. Would you be willing to share some of your memories?"

I was imposing on Mrs. Andō, but summer homework had created a valuable opportunity.

Mrs. Katsura Andō was wearing a modest dress and wore her silver hair in a perm. She looked like an older woman that you might see anywhere.

She looked at me with some surprise, but she soon invited me in.

She showed me to a combined living room and altar room that faced a wide, enclosed porch. I could see a yard full of trees outside.

"I went down to Tokyo to spend the New Year's holiday with my son," Mrs. Andō told me. "I fell and injured myself and had to stay in the hospital. It took much longer than I expected to heal, and it was June by the time I came back. I did not hear of Mr. Sada's death until recently, and I felt terribly rude for not having paid my respects. I went to light some incense at your place right away. Mr. Sada was my supervisor at work, until he retired, and his generosity helped me immensely."

Mrs. Andō seemed to be repeating information she had shared with my mother.

"Was my grandfather scary to work for?" I asked. Grandpa had been a silent type, so I wondered if his colleagues liked him very much.

"He was a man of few words. Nonetheless, Mr. Sada had a big heart—"

Mrs. Andō glanced at her family's altar. I looked at it too.

Aaa—! I almost gasped aloud.

Two photos stood on the altar. One of them showed a young man, and the other showed Akari. She even had the same red baubles in her hair.

Mrs. Andō saw me looking at the photos and added, "That was my daughter. She was in the hospital for a very long time. She died when she was ten, almost forty years ago."

So Akari was not her granddaughter. Akari was Mrs. Andō's daughter, who had died four decades before.

"When I visited Mr. Sada's house and prayed at your altar, Kazu, I was also thinking about Saori, that was my daughter's name. Since Saori was hospitalized a lot, I often had to miss work or leave early. It was hard to ask permission from my superiors, but Mr. Sada understood. My husband had died young, so I had to support my family. I truly appreciated Mr. Sada's kindness. Every Christmas, he would even give me toys and cute stuffed animals to give to Saori. He gave me presents for her older brother too; your grandfather must have realized he would feel left out if only Saori were getting gifts. Mr. Sada told me that his wife enjoyed picking out lovely things for a girl, because they only had boys in the house."

Mrs. Andō smiled and looked at a row of faded stuffed animals, which were lined up in front of a bookshelf on the enclosed porch. I guessed she must not have been able to throw her daughter's things away, even after all these years.

She had a kindly look in her eyes. It seemed she was able to talk of her daughter without tears now. Perhaps she had already cried enough for a lifetime.

"Saori had a short life without much joy in it," she went on. "I so wished that I could bring her back with a healthy body! I prayed for this with all my might. I remembered that prayer when I visited your house."

That's it! I thought. That was why Akari had returned! I wanted to scream it right there in Mrs. Andō's house.

"If Saori had lived just a few more years, she might have survived due to advances in medicine," Mrs. Andō continued. "I couldn't help thinking that, even though it's been so long."

After speaking in a kind of reverie, Mrs. Andō seemed to come back to herself. She looked at me in apology.

I longed to tell her that Saori-chan *had* come back, as Akari Shinobu. But I wasn't sure if I should tell her. Perhaps I should do it later, I thought, after I understood the situation more clearly. For now, I kept quiet.

The Mr. Sada that Mrs. Andō described sounded a bit different from the grandpa I knew. He had been kind to my family and me, of course, but I never knew that he showed that kindness to others as well. Knowing this made me glad. I said thank you, and then I left Mrs. Andō's house. I began to think that a project about my grandpa might not be so bad.

The previous night and this morning had been amazing. I'd figured out quite a lot about Kimyō Temple, and I had even learned something about Akari's past.

Everything had been such a coincidence. Mrs. Andō had prayed for Saori's return at the statuette at our house, without knowing our house was Kimyō Temple. Saori had wanted to come back, of course. It made sense—she'd been stuck in a hospital for most of her life.

I decided then and there to keep Akari's story quiet. I would keep it to myself for the rest of my life. I was actually glad that I hadn't had a chance to tell Yūsuke. I vowed to make sure that Saori, as Akari Shinobu, would get to enjoy her new life as a healthy person. I would help her so she would never feel anxious. And I would do it so she would never know that I knew her story. Which made me begin to wonder if I could pull it off.

I also got to thinking about a movie my sister had told me about. In it, a murdered girl returned from the grave to take revenge on her killer. I also remembered a *rakugo* storytelling performance I had seen with Uncle Junichi about a man who had promised never to remarry when his wife died, but then got married again after some years passed. The dead wife came back as a ghost to express her displeasure.

Maybe Akari also had certain things she wanted to do, or something she wanted to say, and that was why she was back. If she wanted to see her real mother, I could help them meet. There were plenty of things that I could do for her.

As I rode my bike home from Mrs. Andō's house, I felt a smile spread across my face.

But I had forgotten something. I had forgotten the number one most important thing that I needed to do.

CHAPTER FIVE

The Missing Statuette

"**I**'m home!"

My mom's "hi" echoed from the living room.

"I'm starving! Mom, what's for lunch?"

"Oh, boy. Now that you're out of school, I need to make your lunches too, don't I?"

Mom walked into the kitchen from the altar room holding a tray, which held one of the teacups we use for guests. We had had a visitor.

"This August will be the first Obon season since your grandpa died, so we'll have more people coming to call. I'll have to go buy things to give as thank-you gifts . . ." Mom talked to herself as she washed the teacup in the sink.

"Mom! My lunch!"

"I hear you. I was thinking we'd have cold noodles with cucumber and ham, but you look like you can't wait. So, instant ramen it is. What flavor do you want? Miso? Soy sauce?"

"Mo-om, it's hot as an oven outside! Do we have to eat hot ramen?"

"Picky, picky! Remember who stands at the stove to boil it, young man. Unless you want to do it yourself?"

Oh, I did not. I bowed and scraped to avoid this fate.

Mom was right about my being too picky. I was lucky I could even eat instant ramen. When Akari was in the hospital all that time, I bet she never got to try instant ramen or convenience store lunches. Again, I was thinking of Akari.

Dripping sweat, I began to slurp the noodles Mom had just made.

"Ms. Minakami was praising you to the skies, you know," she told me. "She called you 'the nicest little boy.' Imagine, you, a 'little boy'!" Mom laughed.

"Ms. Minakami—you mean Ms. Minakami from Minami Heights?" I asked.

Mom nodded.

"Where did you see her? Was she just here? Why did she come?" I got a sinking feeling.

"Yes, she just visited," Mom answered. "She was early."

"Early for what?"

"For Obon, the celebration of the ancestors. Ms. Minakami said that she has other plans during Obon in August and can't come here then."

"Really? You mean people will come *again* and pay their respects to Grandpa?"

"So it seems. Our relatives will for sure. We may also have people from the neighborhood, and others who knew your grandpa well. When your grandma died, your grandpa took care of all this, so I'm not certain of the details. But I'm glad I at least put the Obon altar lanterns out. Ms. Minakami brought an offering of money, so I'll have to buy her a present to express gratitude. Oh, and I need to clean inside the altar—I can't exactly stick the vacuum hose in there. I wonder why she looked at it so closely . . ."

"Aa—!"

I sprang up with my chopsticks in my hand. This was no time to be snarfing ramen.

I ran to the altar room. I hadn't checked for the Kimyō Temple statuette! I didn't even know what it looked like. Uncle Junichi only said that it would be on the altar. It dawned on me that I hadn't bothered to see if it was still there.

My family's altar is old and big. It has a main cabinet with a long, skinny table in front. At both ends of the table we usually have vases with flowers in them. Today there were also some special Obon lanterns, which my mom had put out; they were turned on, with the lights rotating in circles. A fancy gold cloth covered the altar table, and on it sat a gold meditation bell, an incense stand, candleholders, matches, and a lighter. The scent of the incense Ms. Minakami had lit still lingered in the air. I saw three or four boxes of sweets stacked near the altar. When the summer and year-end gift-giving seasons come, my family always places the gifts we get near the altar first—even bottles of cooking oil or boxes of laundry soap.

Yūsuke and I grew up in houses with altars, so this all seems normal to us, but once I had a friend come over who lives in an apartment, and he was shocked to see us fetching snacks from our altar. The only part of the altar I'm truly familiar with, though, is the area around it. I've never looked carefully inside it. When I tried to peer into the main cabinet, the table in front of it blocked my way, so I scooted the table over and looked more closely.

The inside of the cabinet must have been gold at one point, but it had faded to light brown. In the middle stood a tall, thin structure like a house with its door open. Inside that structure stood a kind of platform, which held a statuette of the Buddha that was maybe a foot tall. Around the Buddha's house stood seven smaller houses with similar doors, and these held memorial tablets for my ancestors. I saw my grandma and grandpa's photos there too. In addition, there were flowers in small vases on each side, two candles in holders, two small gold cups (shaped like trophies) for offering rice, two melons, my grandpa's old teacup filled with water, and a few other items. The cabinet was pretty cluttered.

I couldn't tell which object was the Kimyō Temple statuette. Was it the Buddha in the center? I didn't see anything that looked exactly right. Mom had said that Ms. Minakami carefully inspected inside the altar, but was that all she had done?

I hurried back to the kitchen and asked her. "Mom, did you ever leave Ms. Minakami alone in the altar room?"

"Did I leave her alone? Yes, I guess I did. I went out to prepare tea and sweets, and then I went back in."

"Did you notice anything missing from the altar?"

"What would be missing?" Mom looked at me curiously.

I could tell that she would be of no help. She made the daily ritual offerings of rice, but she hadn't memorized the altar's contents.

I fired off another email to Uncle Junichi.

What does the statuette look like?

I kicked myself for not asking that in the first place. I had no idea what I might be looking for. It could be a likeness of the Buddha. Then again, it could be a stone. It could be a mirror like in a Shinto shrine. My mom had offered rice and water near it every day but hadn't noticed it missing, so it couldn't be that big. If there had been two large Buddhas and one had disappeared, Mom would have noticed. The statuette had been passed to different households, so it must have been the right size to fit in many different altars. And it would have to be small enough that Ms. Minakami could snatch it without Mom seeing. As I waited for Uncle Junichi's reply, I felt certain that Ms. Minakami was a thief.

My uncle's reply arrived more quickly than I expected. Since I had emailed him the night before, he had apparently begun missing home and started emailing with friends in Japan. He said he had a little more time to sit at the computer now than before. He wrote:

It's a Buddha statuette made of ebony. The statuette and the structure around it are small enough to sit on the palm of your hand. It's about four inches tall. What's wrong? Is it not there?

I wrote back to him:

It's gone.

I wanted to tell him so much more—and that Ms. Minakami had swiped it.

Look again! Uncle Junichi replied. We had it in the altar, but it was kind of behind the memorial tablets for my mom and dad.

I replied: I did look closely.

He asked: Why would it be missing?

I replied: I have no idea.

Ms. Minakami stole it, I thought to myself.

Uncle Junichi replied to me.

Well, find it! If the statuette disappears, the power of Kimyō Temple disappears with it. And if—if—there are people who have come back to life through Kimyō Temple, those people could disappear too.

Akari's life was in danger!

Got it!

That was all I could say back to him.

Ms. Minakami must have figured out from watching me that someone had returned to life through Kimyō Temple. She had suspected the statuette was in my house. She had come to check it out. And she had taken the ebony Buddha.

Why would she do that? *Why?* I needed answers.

I found myself back at Minami Heights apartment 902, face-to-face with Ms. Minakami and Kiriko.

To my annoyance, Ms. Minakami offered me food. "Kazu, I know you're fond of watermelon. Your mother told me! I just ordered some from the greengrocer, and it arrived a few minutes ago. It isn't cold yet, but would you like some?"

The watermelon she put on my plate was lukewarm and gross.

I was sure she knew I would come and had lain in wait. That had to be proof of a crime.

I poked at the watermelon but got down to business. "You took a Buddha statuette from our altar," I blurted out. "Please give it back."

"My, my, how rude you are, young man! What are you talking about? I don't know a thing about a statuette."

Ms. Minakami opened her eyes wide. She could really be dramatic.

"You're the only person who *could* know," I said, glaring back at her. I did not look down. For me, this was really saying something.

Ms. Minakami stayed silent a moment, but then she shrugged. "You realize, don't you, that you have no proof?"

"How could you *do* that?"

"I told you, I've done nothing!"

"*Nyaaa!*" Even Kiriko joined the chorus.

This conversation was going nowhere. Ms. Minakami realized it too. She leaned uncomfortably close to me.

"Listen, young man, let's say I did steal the statuette. Leaving aside whether I would even *do* that, don't you think it's wrong that the dead should come back to life?"

"I don't think it's wrong at all," I replied.

"Oh, *really* . . . so you're saying it's fine to have ghosts running around."

"Of course! What's bad about that?" Even I was surprised by how quickly and clearly I answered.

"But it's unfair!" she argued. "Everybody in this world gets one lifetime, Kazu. One chance. We all try to live in such a way that we have no regrets. Some of us may still end up disappointed, of course. That's how it goes. But, 'Oh, I wanted to do this,' 'Oh, I wanted to do that'—having regrets when we die is part of living. Every single one of us must face that fact. There's no way I would choose to return to life after I died," Ms. Minakami finished, nodding for emphasis.

"But wouldn't you be happy if you could come back and have a new start?" I asked her.

"I might be. But still, it wouldn't do. People have to live as if there is no second chance—so they'll make the most of every day. That, my dear, is how I live my life."

"That might be fine for people who grow old, but—"

"Stop your nonsense! I'm eighty-three." Ms. Minakami shook her head as if to say she was nowhere near old.

She had lived plenty long as it was, in my opinion, but I didn't say that. I kept my mouth shut. But she read my thoughts.

"Aha! I see. You're thinking of people who aren't 'old ladies' like I am, hmm? If someone your age passed away, I can see why there would be many things a person still wanted to do." Ms. Minakami nodded knowingly.

I wanted to click my tongue in disgust at myself. I might as well have told her that the person who returned was a child! If we kept going like this, the whole secret of Akari's identity would slip out. All because I had rushed over here without thinking first. I needed to get away. I started to stand up.

Ms. Minakami stopped me with her eyes. What an exasperating granny! Kiriko too—she used her cat eyes to say, *Stay where you are, or else.* How pitiful was this? I sighed deeply as I sank back into the sofa.

"Listen, Kazu. Everyone says that humans are equal, but we don't all get the same chances in life. You know that, don't you? You're a big boy in fifth grade. Some people are born healthy, and others are born with illnesses and disabilities. There are beautiful people who get adored by everyone, and people of fine character who never get any credit due to their looks. Some children get good grades without studying, while others study like crazy for nothing. Plenty of things in this world are not fair and equal, Kazu."

I'd never thought about this, but I found myself nodding at Ms. Minakami's words. I always insist that I'm fine being third, but I also think that if I'd been a little faster on my feet, I could have kept playing baseball.

"But one thing is the same for everyone, Kazu. Not only on the surface, but through and through," Ms. Minakami went on. "It affects the smart people, the rich people—no matter what they do, they cannot get more of it than their due. Do you know what I'm referring to?"

Of course I didn't. I glared at the air in front of me.

"Time, Kazu. Time is the same for everyone. Men, women, young people, old people—everyone. A day is a day. An hour is an hour. Time is the one thing applied impartially to all humans, and to every living creature. This is something we must protect.

"And yet, there are people who try to recapture time when it's gone." Ms. Minakami pursed her lips. "Don't you think that's unfair?"

I could see what she meant. But I didn't agree.

"I don't think it's unfair, exactly . . . I mean, maybe we don't need to be so harsh on people," I said. "If someone wants a second chance and that chance is available, why not take it? It's like the lottery—some people get lucky, some people don't, and—"

I couldn't say it how I wanted.

"You're talking about luck," she replied.

"What do you mean?" I asked.

"Kazu, did you hear about Kimyō Temple from your grandfather?" Ms. Minakami asked. She had used the words 'Kimyō Temple' for the first time.

"No," I said, shaking my head. "I heard it from Uncle Junichi." But in truth, he had sounded like he wasn't sure himself.

"Do you know why Kimyō Temple faded away?" Ms. Minakami asked.

"Something about the anti-Buddhist movement in the Meiji Period."

That was what Uncle Junichi's email had said.

"Actually, they say it was because there were people who misused it."

"Misused?"

"Misused. Think about it—people can come back to life!"

I nodded.

"Dying is scary for everyone. Coming back seems like a good idea."

I nodded again.

"Some people asked folks to pray for them at Kimyō Temple, so they would come back to life," Ms. Minakami went on. "They also asked people to search for them once they returned, to find them in their new families.

"And there were keepers of Kimyō Temple who accepted money for this service, in secret."

"They made it a business."

Even I could see the problem with that.

Uncle Junichi said he thought it was fishy that the returned souls went to new families, but I had liked that part of it. I liked the idea that people would set all thoughts of themselves and their families aside and pray purely for someone's second chance. That selfless affection had brought people back. And the people who returned, even if they were anxious like Akari, would do everything they could to make the best of their new lives. That side of Akari had made me want to help her. But now I was hearing that people had taken money for this. I felt let down.

"It was a fake temple—no, not fake exactly. But it became corrupt," Ms. Minakami said. "It made people move away from our street, and it made people hunt down the returned spirits."

They pointed fingers and said, "Child of Kimyō Temple!" Even I might do that, if I knew someone had paid money to rig a second chance at life.

"And at some point, the statuette disappeared from Kimyō Temple Alley. Spirits stopped coming back to life.

My ancestors were on the side that helped snuff out the returned ones," said Ms. Minakami. "My family believed that the statuette needed to disappear. They believed that Kimyō Temple had no place in this world. They told their children to hide its history and to keep watch, so it would never be misused again.

"They worried that it would come back—probably because they didn't know if the statuette was really gone. I learned this from my parents. I didn't believe it. Who, honestly, would believe it?" Ms. Minakami said. "I figured that even if Kimyō Temple once existed, the statuette was burned in the anti-Buddhist movement."

She looked at me as if to say, *But now I know . . .*

"My ancestors hid the statuette," I told her.

"I thought as much when you said you were researching Kimyō Temple. I was shocked! The neighborhood association president, the priest at Ryūseiji, and I—we've all tried to keep Kimyō Temple a secret for years! We try not to let the young folks find out. If we discovered a returned spirit among us, we would snuff it out, too, I'm pretty certain. We see it as our duty. Until recently, though, I figured your family also helped to eliminate the ghosts."

"My ancestors may have done that," I said, "but I think they believed that Kimyō Temple had a place in this world."

Uncle Junichi believed that. And I believed it. At this moment, I was speaking as a bearer of the Sada name.

"Well, there you have it," said Ms. Minakami. "Our thinking is different. My beliefs and your beliefs—that is to say, your ancestors' beliefs—are different."

I nodded to agree.

"Not much we can do about that." Ms. Minakami nodded too.

"So would you please give me the statuette back?" I said.

"*What* statuette?" Ms. Minakami said, all innocent.

She had zero plans to admit that she had taken the Buddha. She was going to treat it like a myth, to the bitter end.

"My family has a right to its beliefs. Please return it."

"I wouldn't take things from your house, young man."

Ms. Minakami shook her head and looked at me peculiarly. Her eyes had the same disconcerting stare as Kiriko's.

I didn't know what more to say. I was the bad one—the one who had failed to protect the statuette. Still, I battled to the last:

"You're despicable," I yelled, "A criminal!"

"That statuette belonged to all families in Kimyō Temple Alley," Ms. Minakami replied. "It even circulated to my own family, generations ago. I know this only through stories, but I'm just saying. Anyway. Kazu, it was with your family quite long enough. You stopped circulating it as you should, and now it has landed in the Minakami household. You may as well think of it like that."

Ms. Minakami grinned widely. She had as good as told me that she had the Buddha, but there was nothing I could do about it. I couldn't search the premises.

"What do you plan to do with it?" I asked.

"If I even *have* it, you mean. Hmm, let's see. What could I do? Since I don't believe it should exist, I could throw it away.

Then again, it might still have power. I wonder if I could burn it the way they do outdated amulets."

"*What!*" I shouted.

"If I even *have* it, I'm saying," she said back. "But if the statuette were destroyed, I wonder what would become of the people who returned? The people who came back decades ago? Their children, and their grandchildren? I wonder what would happen to them?"

She furrowed her brows. Uncle Junichi had told me that the returned spirits could be snuffed out if the statuette were destroyed. Ms. Minakami obviously thought the same thing. "I suppose if the statuette left this world, then those who've returned would leave this world too," she said. She rubbed her arm as if she had goose bumps.

"If there *were* people who had come back . . . Kazu, do you know any?"

I nearly nodded.

"Well, I'm not asking you to tell me," she said. "I have no need to know. After all, those people would change or disappear anyway!"

She planned to burn the statuette! She might have done so already! My mind raced.

"Did you burn it?" I asked.

She didn't answer clearly. I panicked.

"H—how? How could you do such a thing? To people who've come all this way back, who are finding joy and magic in every little thing—" I stood up without realizing it.

"Well, now, you're right. They did come all this way. It seems fair to let them enjoy it while they still can. Even I am not a monster, you know." Ms. Minakami gave a modest smile for show.

While they still can? What was she saying? Was there still time?

"You haven't burned it yet then, have you?" I said.

"Now *listen*, Kazu-kun. How could I burn something I don't have?" she replied.

I couldn't take it anymore. "Just *tell* me!!" I yelled.

"OK, you're right. It won't be tomorrow. Even I don't know exactly when. Three days from now? A week? It's only a legend after all."

Was she declaring that even though the statuette had disappeared, it wouldn't be destroyed right away?

"I wonder what those ghosts wish to do with their second chance?" she went on. "I hope it's something that won't disturb other people. There are spirits who want to do bad things, you know—spirits who've frightened people, cursed them, sought revenge . . . it's awful! Though I suppose you can't wipe out grudges." She nodded as if even she could sympathize.

Then she said, "Well, I'll see you later."

I heard Ms. Minakami's voice below me. That's when I knew I was standing.

She was telling me to leave. Kiriko had curled into a ball in the corner of the sofa and was no longer even looking at me. I got angry, but I worried for Akari. I wondered if she had any time left. I wondered if she had already disappeared before she could do much of anything with her second chance.

~~~~

I zoomed from Minami Heights to Akari's place.

Her house was still there, so maybe she had not vanished. But a house was one thing, Akari another. I couldn't remember if the house had really been there before Akari showed up.

Without thinking, I pressed the doorbell.

"Co-oming!" sang a voice. She was there!

"It's Kazu. Kazu Sada!" I shouted.

The door opened. No one stood there.

I froze. My panicked brain was no longer responding.

"Hello, Kazu! Did you come to see Akari?" A voice spoke from above me and to one side.

It was Akari's invisible mother. I'd forgotten about her until I heard her speak. I no longer felt remotely in my right mind, but I processed that if her mother was still here, Akari must still be around too.

"Uh. Uhmm." I wasn't sure which way to look, so I stared in the direction Invisible Mama's voice had come from and forced myself to smile. "Is Akari at home?"

"She went to the bookstore. Something about having to write a book report for summer homework. Have you decided on your book, Kazu?"

"Umm, was that an assignment?" I had forgotten.

"Oh, Kazu, that's so like you!" Invisible Mama began to laugh.

I shivered. It seemed as if she knew me from way before too.

"I'll go look for Akari at the bookstore," I said.

I planned to peek inside the store and see if Akari was all right. I knew I couldn't relax until I saw her and her red baubles with my own eyes.

"I think she went to the store in M building," Akari's mom said. "We stopped at the one on the way back from the Kannon temple yesterday, but they didn't have what she was looking for."

"OK, I understand. Thank you!" I said. I directed my words to roughly where I thought she would be. Invisible Mama was friendly.

Akari hadn't gone to two bookstores in Minami Ōdori, but to the M building near our train station, which has lots of businesses inside, including a used bookstore.

She hadn't disappeared yet. Now I needed to know what she wanted to do with the time she had left. She might not have long. She had come all this way, and I wanted her to feel at least a little bit glad she had returned.

I stopped by my house and grabbed my bike. I pointed it toward the station and had just started to pedal when I saw red baubles heading my way. It was Akari. She really hadn't disappeared!

"Akari! He-e-y, Akari!" I was so relieved that I called to her loudly.

"Oh, Kazu-kun."

Akari saw me and stood still, making a strange face. I jumped off my bike in front of her. I must have had a crazed expression.

I wanted to apologize, saying, "I'm sorry. I let somebody steal the statuette!" But I swallowed the words.

If her true identity stayed secret, and no one called her a child of Kimyō Temple, maybe she could live for a little while. Or so it seemed. I only knew about Kimyō Temple through hearsay. I didn't know anything for sure. Even Ms. Minakami had been vague. All of it was conjecture. Maybe it was better not to say a word about the temple or the statuette. If I said something the wrong way, after all, Akari could lose everything. What *should* I say? Again, I'd rushed into everything too quickly. I needed to look before I leaped. I sighed.

"So, umm." In the end, that was what came out of my mouth. Totally lame.

"Umm," Akari echoed. She probably wondered what I could possibly want.

She turned bright red.

Oh no! She had the wrong idea. She thought I was about to tell her I liked her. What a mess.

"Umm, sorry. It's not that. It's . . ." I had no clue what to say. "Anyway, do you want to go someplace cooler? Maybe the Kannon temple grounds?"

"OK."

I started to push my bicycle, Akari walking beside me.

I had forgotten we were in front of Takamatsuya, Yūsuke's store. My brain had shut off.

When your timing is bad, everything else gets even worse. Who should come out of the Takamatsuya alley just then, but the boy who should have been in bed with a tummy ache. Yūsuke glanced over, took one look at me and Akari, and jumped to conclusions.

"Oh. Kazu, Akari."

I couldn't take this anymore. I no longer cared what happened.

"Is your stomach better? See you later then," I said. I waved my hand and moved on.

Yūsuke's face was priceless. It gave "thunderstruck" a whole new meaning.

Akari and I headed to the temple grounds.

It really did seem like I'd asked her on a date. I'd never gone out with a girl before. This was my first time. Hmm, my very first date was with a ghost. In the heat I began to wither like dried-up grass. Maybe "freeze up" is more the term.

I looked around, hoping I wouldn't see anyone I knew in the temple yard, but I only saw a grandmother playing with her grandchild.

Akari and I sat on a bench under a tree. Next to me, Akari blushed and began to sweat. Honestly, it would have been easier just to say, "I like you."

Settle down! I told myself. I breathed deeply. I had to let Akari know that the statuette was gone. Tell her that her life might fade away. But I had no idea where to start. I sighed out loud for the zillionth time.

Akari stole a look at me, but after that she smiled and watched the little girl, who was about three years old, jumping and splashing in the ritual handwashing area. For a moment, I thought Akari looked more like a grandma than a girl. *Wait a minute, that's right,* I thought. If she had lived, she wouldn't quite be a grandma yet, but she would be a

middle-aged woman. She was ten years old now, but her eyes looked different from mine and the other kids. She seemed to take pleasure in whatever she saw. Akari had come back to life! She had problems, sure, but everything she saw and heard and felt must seem so interesting, so exciting—she must hardly be able to stand it!

I had no clue how to apologize to her. I wanted to think carefully before I spoke. At the same time, I had to get out of this odd situation, and the sooner the better. I had a dilemma.

"Is there anything you want to do? Anything you want to do right now?" I asked, feeling relieved that I didn't sound too stupid.

Akari grimaced. She must have expected me to say I liked her.

"Is there anything you want to do? Really!" I persisted.

"I want to become a doctor," she answered. With her eyes, she followed the little girl as she slipped from her grandma's hands and ran around.

A doctor. It made sense. Akari had been in the hospital and had probably admired her pediatrician. I nodded to show I understood. But somehow, I had to tell her that she had run out of time to become an adult. And the whole thing was my fault. If I could just come clean to her now, I knew I would feel much better. At the same time, I didn't know if I had the right to apologize to her—to apologize would be to reveal her true condition. If I did that, Akari might disappear right here and now.

"I—I don't mean so far in the future. I mean, is there anything you'd like to do at this very moment? Something you have to do, no matter what? Ah, I don't know how to say it." I pawed at my hair in frustration.

Akari looked at me questioningly.

I tried again. "Like, uh, if you knew you were going to die tomorrow, what would you want to do today?"

Now I was the one who wanted to vanish.

"What on earth?" Akari tried to laugh as if she had never even considered such a thing.

And then, Akari's eyes went dark.

CHAPTER SIX

Daisy

"**K**azu, you're not just making conversation, are you?"
Akari's face crumpled.

I was sure she was about to cry, and I could only sit there paralyzed, opening and closing my mouth like a goldfish.

"I was so happy—I had so many plans, Kazu, I was determined to do my best! But it's not going to happen, is it?"

Akari practically ground her teeth trying to hold in her disappointment. Then she began to weep quietly.

I had worried about what to do if she cried, but watching her sob silently was so much worse than I had imagined.

Akari had come all this way, and now her hopes were being dashed again. She ought to be sobbing much harder, I thought. She ought to be screaming and stamping her feet and wailing! That would have been easier for me to take.

She had imagined a future where she finished grade school, went on to middle school and high school, graduated from university and became a doctor, got married, and had a family. I had just stomped all over those dreams. Maybe I shouldn't have spoken. Maybe I should have let her disappear while still believing, still certain that she could live her dreams. Maybe she would have been happier that way. I didn't think of that until she was right in front of me. I should have considered all this right after I checked on Invisible Mama. I felt like such an idiot—always rushing, always forgetting to think. I wanted to kick myself.

"I didn't come here to tell you, you know—*that*," I said. Silently, I begged Akari to understand. I had no intention of revealing her true nature or snuffing her out with the deadly phrase. I didn't even want to risk saying the words *Kimyō Temple* out loud. She didn't have to fear that from me. But I wasn't sure if she understood.

Akari wiped her eyes and looked at me searchingly. She considered what I had said.

"The other day at school, I thought, oh no. Kazu knows," she said. "But I understood. I came back through your house, after all.

"When you pointed me out, I thought everything might be all over in just one day. But then it was fine. I was fine. I began to think, maybe I'd make it."

She was talking about multigrade activity time, when I had ranted that she was a ghost. She had acted like she didn't notice, but inside she had been panicking. She could stay alive only as long as no one called her a "child of Kimyō Temple"—and as long as the statuette was safe.

"Look, I'm not going to say those words, OK? You can relax about that," I said.

Akari looked at me with a concerned expression of "so what's wrong then?"

"But I did do something that amounts to the same thing, Akari. I let someone steal the statuette. Someone who wants to destroy it. I begged for it back, but it didn't work. The person who stole it might even burn it. I am so sorry. You came all this way! I feel awful."

This time I started to cry, which surprised me.

Akari looked at me and said, simply: "So, it'll be soon."

"Yeah, I'm pretty sure. I don't know when, exactly. But soon. I don't think you'll have time to become a doctor, Akari. So . . . if you assume there won't be a tomorrow, is there anything—"

"I'm the one who's sorry, Kazu."

"You have nothing to apologize for!" I said.

"But you cried, Kazu, and it's my fault." She seemed to feel horrible.

"What I feel doesn't matter at all, Akari. What do you want to do? If there's anything I can do to help, I will!"

I scolded myself that this was no time to sit here blubbering. The only one who had any right to cry was Akari.

"I've been so happy that I've really only thought about my future," she muttered, dazed. "I really can't think of things I want to do right now."

I was disappointed, but I knew that what Akari said made sense. A ghost who wanted to identify her murderer or haunt her former lover was the stuff of movies and rakugo.

Akari was ten when she died, and she had been in the hospital for most of her life. Her wish must simply have been to come back healthy.

"Is there anyone that you want to see? Like your mom?"

I could help her meet Mrs. Andō. I wanted to take her right away.

"I don't remember my former family."

"You don't even remember who you were before?"

Akari shook her head.

"Your name was Saori Andō, and you died of illness forty years ago," I wanted to tell her. But I kept quiet. It wasn't my place to reveal such sad things. I had gotten us in enough trouble by acting impulsively.

"I don't think about meeting my former family," she said. "It must be because I don't remember them."

So it was true that when families prayed to Kimyō Temple, their loved ones came back as different people. I liked that. It meant that those who prayed really were not praying for themselves, but to give their loved ones a chance to live again. A temple with that kind of power should have a place in the world.

"But my feelings are the same as they were before," Akari continued. "I couldn't do anything in my old life, so I was bored. I wanted to go to school, and I wanted to make friends and chat with them, and I wondered why I had to be sick. I was disappointed and sad and depressed at having to leave the people I loved. It's like I stayed in that sad state for a very long time, in a dark place . . ."

"Oh, I see. I wonder if that's how it is for all the people who come back?"

"I think it must be. And that's why they can make the journey." Akari nodded confidently.

I knew she was right. The more unfulfilled and denied a spirit felt, the harder it would hope to return.

"So, when you got back here, you decided to be a doctor," I said.

"That's right. I went to school. I found out what a school smells like, and what school lunch tastes like. Even summer homework was exciting—like, wow, I've made it! This is it!"

Akari put both fists under her chin and struck a pose like an old-fashioned TV star.

"I was so thrilled that I could wear a yukata and go to the summer festival. I don't even know how to spend a summer vacation properly. Should I go to the beach? I figure I'll just watch what everyone else does carefully. 'Cause I'm on my own, in a way. Oh, Kazu, you know that, too, right?"

"Yeah, I know. Weird, isn't it?" I knew she meant Invisible Mama.

"The morning I came back, I was standing in front of your altar. Then there was this woman beside me—a voice. She said, 'Welcome back, Akari-chan.' That was when I realized, ah, my name is Akari. And she took me to that house."

When Akari had left my house, Invisible Mama had been there too. I'd been watching from the second floor, so I couldn't hear her voice. Now I knew that Akari was as alone as I thought—and that Invisible Mama appeared transparent to her too. I was shocked all over again.

"There's nothing in your house, is there?" I asked.

"Nothing at all. You saw for yourself, Kazu. You're the only one who knows the truth. My mom manages everything so that no one thinks anything is off. She'll go and buy food for supper, without me saying anything. If she meets someone from the neighborhood on the way, she'll stop and greet them as if they've known each other for years! Everyone else can see her fine." Akari made her eyes bulge.

"She's not the only strange thing," I said. "Everyone else talks about you like they've known you forever. Everyone but me. Until I heard about Kimyō Temple, I thought that there was something wrong with me. I was worried."

"You must have been! You've been dealing with all this from the completely opposite side," Akari said. "I've been worried, too, Kazu, just trying to figure out how to live from day to day. When Mom took me to my house, there was nothing inside . . . All I saw was a desk on the second floor, in what I guessed must be my room. A bed and linens only appeared at nightfall. A backpack showed up on the desk chair labeled Akari Shinobu, Uchimaru Elementary School, Grade 5 Section 1. There were some textbooks and notebooks laid out. I had no idea what school was like, so I put every single book into the backpack. There was clothing as well. It was exactly the kind I used to think was cute. When I put the clothes on and left the house with my backpack the next day, I wasn't so much happy as nervous—my heart almost went flying out of my mouth. I followed everybody else to get to school. I didn't know if my dress was OK, because the other girls seemed to have skirts with leggings underneath. My fashion sense is decades old, I guess. Plus, I used to wear pajamas all the time.

"Anyway, that first morning, somebody called out 'hi' to me, and I almost jumped out of my skin! I didn't know who the person was. When I looked at her nametag, it said she was in my class. So, I said 'hi' back and went to school with her. When I got to the classroom, I didn't know which seat was mine, so I sort of stood there lost for a while. I told the person who had walked with me that I had to go to the bathroom, and I asked her to take my bag. When I came back, the bag was on my chair, and that's how I figured out where to sit.

"Seriously, that first day I was so tense, Kazu! My heart was pounding the whole time. The moment you singled me out was the worst, I think. But even then, I didn't disappear. And everybody kept acting as if they knew me from before. So, I just kept doing what everyone else did and somehow got through the day."

Akari's words spilled out. She must have been desperate to confide in someone. I was in awe of her.

"I heard about the summer festival at school," she went on. "I heard the other girls talking about how they were going to go in yukata. When I went home and told my mother that I wanted to go and wear a yukata, she began talking as if she had one already—and there it was! And little by little, furniture began to appear. When I went to take a bath, I found a towel and soap and toiletries. When my mom began to make supper, we had a refrigerator, a rice cooker, a frying pan, dishes, and a table!"

Akari sighed in wonder at it all.

I sighed too. Wow. I had never actually seen the Kimyō Temple statuette, but Uncle Junichi said it was a Buddha icon that would sit in the palm of my hand. I couldn't believe that a tiny statuette had the power to make such amazing things happen.

"But of course it makes sense that magic like that can't last forever. I remember thinking it was all like a dream," Akari said. She had stopped crying. "I guess that's all it actually was."

I wanted to do something for Akari. To make her feel it had been worth it to return.

"Do you want to go to the beach?" I asked her.

A minute ago, she had mentioned going to the seaside since it was summer.

"I've never been to the beach, so I don't know whether it's fun. But I'm sure I would like it."

She nodded decisively, as if convinced that this was so.

"Going to the mountains would be fine too, then?" I asked.

"Yes! Any place would be great so long as I can feel the sun and think, ah, it's summer. Even walking around a bookstore looking for a good story and having a boy in my class call out to me is better than you can imagine!"

"I see, so even right now is fun," I said, starting to think she was messing with me.

"Yes!" Akari nodded. "If I disappeared here and now, I would be disappointed, but I would figure fate is fate. I already got to go to school, and I got to experience a little of summer vacation."

"Wow, you're so strong." That was all I could say.

"I'm not strong at all, Kazu. I'm so used to giving up."

I wanted to tell her to never give up, not in a million years. But I knew it might come out the wrong way. All I could do to help Akari, if Ms. Minakami still had the statuette, was beg and beg her to keep it safe as long as possible. And maybe I could try to ask for it back again, though that was probably useless.

Oh, Ms. Minakami was such a bullheaded granny! Without realizing it, I had clenched my fists. Was there really no way to get the statuette back? Could I kidnap Kiriko and force Ms. Minakami to exchange it for the cat? Maybe, but how would I kidnap the cat? I doubted it would go well. I hung my head. I realized that even if I did that, the statuette could already have been burned. All I could do was sulk.

"Kazu-kun, don't get so discouraged!"

Now Akari was comforting *me*. This was beyond pitiful. I had to pull myself together.

"Do you want to see fireworks?" I suggested.

"Yes, that sounds great!"

All of a sudden, we were chatting away as if everything were normal.

I wanted to show Akari the different types of fireworks: spinners, sparklers, the big local displays.

"We could ask Yūsuke and Ami and her friends to join us," I said.

Akari and I both stood up.

"Didn't you go to buy a book?" I asked, seeing that her hands were empty.

"Yes, but they didn't have what I was looking for."

"Was it on a list or something?"

"No, just something I've been wanting to read for ages . . ."

"Ages—you mean, since before?"

"Yes, that's right. Oh! Kazu! Yes! There's a story I want to read!"

"A story? What story? Hey, we could get it! Let's get it!"

Akari nodded. She grabbed my hands and we actually started bouncing around. If Yūsuke had seen us, I would never have lived it down.

"It was a story in a magazine called *Daisy*," she said when we stood still again. "It was printed as a serial; each issue of *Daisy* had a new section of the story."

"Is that why you went to the used bookstore?"

"Yes. But no luck." Akari looked down.

"A magazine . . . yeah, that's hard. It would have been issues from years ago."

I had been to the used bookstore too. They had tons of paperback and hardback books, but not many weekly or monthly magazines.

"Oh! But what if after the story came out in the magazine, it became a book? They do that sometimes with manga," I said, getting excited. "They make a paperback. What was the story called?"

"It was called 'The Moon Is on the Left.'"

I'd never heard of it. I don't really read many books.

"I asked the bookseller to search for it by title, but nothing came up," Akari said.

"Who's the author?"

"I can't remember. It might have been a foreign name."

"I see. So, you've only got the title to go on."

It seemed the story might be hard to find. Here we'd finally hit on something she wanted to do, but I was going to be of no help again. I hung my head.

"Kazu!" Akari admonished. "Stop moping. I've only been here three days, but look! I've got a friend! That alone makes me happy. I never had a friend I could talk to like this, you know."

She smiled and skipped off. I guessed that would be all for now.

I stared at her back. I figured she had said that to make me feel better. She was happy just to be able to run. She had called me her friend, but I was nothing more than a villain who was ruining her life. She had been back for three days! Less than the life of a cicada. I could tell my eyes were going to fill with tears again.

Then I thought of something. I grabbed my bike and turned in the opposite direction.

I rode to Mrs. Andō's house in Midorigaoka.

Mrs. Andō smiled in recognition when she saw me.

"I, uh, apologize for coming suddenly without phoning first," I said to her. "I have a strange question for you. I wondered—your daughter Saori-chan, did she happen to like a magazine called *Daisy*?"

"Yes! Goodness, yes, she did," Mrs. Andō nodded several times, as if just remembering. "I bought each monthly issue for her the day it came out and took it to the hospital. I glanced inside it once, and it looked like it was for girls a bit older than her, actually. But I kept buying it since she was so keen—"

"Do you still have them?" I cut in. I had no time to lose.

Mrs. Andō nodded that she did.

I wasn't sure if I should ask her to loan them to me. She seemed to sense this. She didn't say that I could borrow any—she had probably kept them in Saori-chan's memory. She might not feel comfortable entrusting them to someone like me. Still, she asked, "Would you like to see the collection?"

I nodded and went inside with her.

"Saori was hospitalized from the age of five, so she didn't really have a room here at home. Here are the magazines."

Mrs. Andō showed me to the bookshelf on the enclosed porch near the family altar. The group of stuffed animals—probably from my grandpa—sat in front of the shelf.

"When I remember how Saori loved to read these, I can't bring myself to throw them away," said Mrs. Andō. She motioned to some faded spines near books that I knew, like the Arséne Lupin books and *Treasure Island*.

I sat on the porch and pulled out the issues of *Daisy*. There were six total. On the covers, girls in styles even I knew were outdated struck cute poses, touching their cheeks with one finger and so on.

Inside, girls who must have been famous back then posed in clothes that were once trendy. I saw a page of horoscopes and an advice column to a reader who had quarreled with her friend. Three different manga stories.

Three fiction stories. The people who made the magazine had thrown in a little of everything. As Mrs. Andō had said, *Daisy* seemed to be for readers older than elementary school.

"The Moon Is on the Left" began in the earliest of the six issues. The pages were yellowed, and the print had faded, but I could still read the text.

Flipping through the pages, I saw that the story had illustrations. The author's name was listed as Mia Lee. Akari had said that the name sounded foreign. Was Mia Lee Chinese, maybe?

I began to read, figuring this would be another story like the ones my sister loves, usually about how two best friends in the same class have a crush on the same person and find themselves in a predicament.

Unexpectedly, I found myself lost in something far more interesting.

Chapter Seven

"The Moon Is on the Left"

PART ONE

I knew that I was going to be sold. My brother, who was a year older, and my sister, who was two years younger, and I, would all be sold. If we stayed at home, there wouldn't be enough food to eat. Father looked sad, but he seemed relieved. There was barely enough food now to feed him, let alone us children.

This would not be the first time Father had sold his children. There were once two half-sisters older than my brother, whom I barely remembered. At some point they had disappeared. People told me they went to work in a far-off town, but now I knew: they too had been sold.

We had no horse to ride. We would have to walk through the forest over a mountain, and then cross a river to reach the capital.

A breeze cooled the summer mountainside. Thinking perhaps it was the least he could do, Father brought out some cheese he'd kept hidden away and smoked rabbit meat for our lunch.

"I've never tasted anything so good!" my sister gushed.

Looking down, we saw a river twine around the base of the mountain, shining like silver cloth. That was the river we would cross. We children had never ridden a boat.

"Will you ride with us, Father? Is it as big as a house?" my sister asked.

"I wonder how it works," my brother mused.

Beyond the boat, I thought of the thick forest on the opposite shore, and the capital that lay beyond, where we would be sold.

By the time we climbed down the mountain, the sun had nearly set.

We hadn't seen them from above, but near the dock stood a cluster of several buildings. Seven or eight stores stood in all, but compared with the solitary house where we lived, the buildings seemed full of life.

Roads led away from the buildings on both sides, apparently to towns. Townspeople assembled here when they wanted to cross the river. Delicious smells wafted out of two restaurants, another store sold water, and still another sold mushrooms and nuts from the mountainside. A fifth sold fish from the river. I saw two inns as well.

Compared with what we had seen above, the river looked frightfully wide. I could not see the opposite bank. If the weather turned bad, and the boat couldn't cross, people bound for the capital would wait in the inns, we were told. The boat was not at the dock.

As we arrived, a wind began to blow, making waves in the river. Four or five people who were also waiting for the boat stared out and said, "It might not come today," nodding to each other in agreement.

But as it began to grow dark, the boat finally arrived. It was large. Some ten people were aboard, and I saw open seats as well. Everyone had to row.

My brother walked warily to the boat and put a foot on it. He turned pale and jumped back when it listed.

We learned it wouldn't depart that night. I expected we would sleep outdoors, but Father led us to the smaller of the two inns.

In the inn's communal room, a number of people had gone to sleep, their bags under their heads as pillows. We found an open space and stretched on the ground.

A man rose abruptly and looked us over. I didn't like his eyes. I could tell he was sizing us up.

"Heading to tomorrow's market?" he asked Father.

Father nodded. Our empty hands told the rest. We had no luggage, no belongings. Clearly what my father had to sell at market was us.

Father and the man talked in low voices in a corner. Father raised a finger, the man raised two, and on they went.

"If we come to an agreement here, you can save on boat fare. I'll make it worth your while." I could hear the man from where I waited. Father must have known this might happen, which was why he paid for an inn.

He returned to us. "This fellow runs a silk operation in the town to the south. He'll take two of you."

Father planned to sell me and my younger sister to him.

I set my jaw and refused. I was sad to part with my sister, but I wished to see the capital. If I did not go now, to be sold, I might never see it my whole life.

"I'll go with him," my brother muttered.

Coward. He feared the boat. I snickered.

My sister didn't seem to care whether my brother or I went with her, so long as she would not be alone. She cried a bit and that was all.

"The boy will be stronger," Father told the man and renegotiated.

⌒

Soon morning came. I walked the road to the boat. My brother and sister walked the road that led south, at the foot of the mountain. We all cried again a little. Just a little.

"It's for the best," Father said, stroking my sister's hair. "You can eat to your heart's content now."

Father himself would eat well after this. I began to feel that I could handle anyplace, so long as it wasn't home.

My brother may have been a coward, but he was no fool. The boat ride made me ill. With the contents of my stomach shifting up, then down—though I had hardly eaten anything—I vomited. I had never felt so wretched. I might not have much meat on my bones, but I had never been sick before.

We disembarked, and I rode from the boat to the capital, through the forest, on Father's back. He worried, but not about me exactly. He worried that my pale face would make me hard to sell.

From Father's back, I saw that the capital was surrounded by a stone wall. No matter how far I tilted my head back, I could not see the top of it. As we passed beneath an archway hewn from the stone, we nearly fell, toppled by pull carts and horse-drawn vehicles. For the first time ever, I saw a stone-paved road. It seemed the capital was surrounded by not one but several walls, including some that had windows. The windows indicated dwellings. Below them on the stone streets, horse carts rolled to and fro, mounted soldiers' horses strutted, and peddlers with packs as tall as they were hurried to market squares along the way.

Against my father's back, I peered about in a daze. I was no longer seasick; now I had so-many-people-I-can't-believe-it sickness.

Father strode down a street and through a gate, and down another street and through another gate. The maze-like streets made the castle hard to reach in the event of an attack, I knew. Our path grew wide and then narrow. We would find ourselves in a square with a well at the center, and then see a steep sloping road or a narrow stairway. One square had a market inside. Vendors sold vegetables, game, furniture, farm tools, and clothing. The buyers wore finer clothes than I had seen in my entire life.

No matter how many gates we passed through, I still could not see the castle. I had heard that it was hidden among these walls. What would a castle look like, and what kind of people lived inside? I let my imagination wander but had no answers.

When Father finally put me down, the sun was high. We had reached a square in the heart of the capital that had a fountain in the middle instead of a well. Around the edges of this square, in place of vendors and their spread of wares, I saw stores lined up in arcades.

Around the fountain, several dozen parents with children to sell were trudging in a circle. The children were like me: skinny, with big eyes, and covered in filth. I slipped in line between a boy who looked younger and a girl who looked older and began to walk with my father. All of the parents had vacant faces, as if they were ready to hand off their children, and yet would never be ready.

Now and then a buyer stepped forward and pointed at a child. The parent would acquire a groveling expression and expound on how the child was strong and sharp.

The buyers wore well-made clothes, had full whiskers, and clutched pouches of money. And they wore shoes. Leather shoes that looked sturdy, with metal rivets.

Those of us who circled the fountain wore cloth shoes. Some had none.

Walking along, dragging our feet, we rounded the fountain countless times. The sun's rays grew stronger, and my unfed body began to feel unsteady. Even so, the number of children had not decreased by half.

We'll trudge around like this forever, I thought. The idea that we might go home did not even occur to me.

"That one."

I heard a woman speak.

"Her name is Adi. She's nine," Father replied. "She's slender but strong and has never had a cold. Tough as nails. She had a younger sister, so she can mind children. She knows her numbers." Father clasped his hands at his chest and held forth.

Sweat ran into my eyes, preventing me from seeing the buyer. Father probably couldn't see either; with the sun behind her, she appeared only as a silhouette. She seemed tall for a woman, and despite the summer heat, she wore a cloak.

"Show me her hands," she said.

I stuck out both hands and heard a murmur of voices: "The woman's a witch, you know. A witch."

I felt large, icy hands grip my own. I pulled back, but the witch made no move to release me.

I had thought I would hardly care who bought me. I had ridden in a boat. I had seen the capital. I figured I could live through whatever came next. I had no dreams. No ambitions. Still, I had never imagined being bought by a witch. I knew there were witches in the world. I had heard they used magic. I also knew that most people feared them.

Now I grew afraid. For the first time, I saw what it meant to be sold to someone I had never met. Fear swallowed me like a wave.

"No! NOOO!"

I fought to free myself and sat down hard on the ground. The witch gripped my hands in one of hers, then reached into the pocket of the dress beneath her cloak. She withdrew a pouch and pushed it at Father.

I sobbed, but I didn't ask Father to help me.

With her free hand, the witch pushed me inside her cloak. It was pitch dark; I could see nothing. Having cried so hard, I couldn't catch my breath. I lost consciousness for the first time ever.

The witch held me to her side and straddled a broom. We soared through the sky. I opened my eyes only once as we flew, and from a gap in the cloak, I

glimpsed the capital's walls. We flew
away from the capital, toward the middle
of a lake that sat in the opposite direction from the
river. A mansion appeared at the edge of the lake,
positioned like a lookout. Around the mansion, hundreds of water birds circled as if to protect it, crying
gyaa-gyaa. The witch's broom headed straight through
the middle of the birds. The speed, and the odd feeling
that my stomach had turned upside down—a different
sensation entirely from the boat—left me unconscious
again.

When I awoke, I found myself on a bed in a small
room. All was quiet. I could not even hear the raucous cries of the birds anymore. The bed was the only
furniture. There was no door in the room's entrance.

The witch spoke. "When you're awake, please come
out."

What would happen to me? Was she planning to eat
me?!

I slid from the bed, and my bare feet landed on
a stone floor polished as carefully as a mirror. My
ripped, soiled shoes had vanished.

The room's doorway led to a larger room like
a hall. Each of its four corners had a

wood burning stove. The stoves were lit. Was it night? The heat of noontime seemed a dream now. My skin felt cool. The flames in the stoves rose tall. The hall had only the four stoves inside—nothing more. To the left stood another doorway with no door in it. The opening revealed darkness. It was indeed night.

"Adi. That's your name, right? I am Stonebird."

I didn't see the witch, but I could hear her speak through the sculpted birds on top of each of the four stoves. The four stone birds were carved with long wings that protected each stove as if it held an egg. The birds had long necks, and their heads all tilted to the same side. Their eyes were open. The witch's voice seemed to come first from one corner and then from another: the right rear bird, then the left front bird.

The hall spooked me. I began to edge toward the exit.

"You can't escape," said the voice from the right rear bird. The eyes of all four birds, eight eyes total, bore into me. My feet stopped as if glued to the floor.

"You have black fingernails, I see," the front right bird said.

"I wonder why?" the right rear bird asked.

I looked at my fingernails. The ends were black. Even when I cut them, they always looked that way, as if mud had soaked into my fingertips. Everyone in my family had such fingernails.

"It's from digging in the mud," I explained.

"Why would you do such a thing?"

I bit my lip. I didn't think of my fingernails as dirty, but I did not want others knowing the details of why my family dug through mud.

Past the cedar grove behind my childhood home, if you climbed through a patch of boulders, you would find a valley of trees with purple flowers that gave off a strong, sweet scent. Hot mud bubbled in that valley. If you breathed its steam for too long, you would get a headache. In the season when the flowers bloomed, people said that their scent mixed with the mud's steam would drive a person mad. I didn't mind the smell of the flowers on its own.

The valley was a burial site. Long ago, before the current royal family assumed power, the capital city stood at the foot of our mountain. The old capital is now a barren field, without even a single blade of grass. My ancestors served its rulers as grave minders. When those rulers died, we no longer had official duties, but our family continued to live by the burial site. We tilled a small field and hunted game from the mountain to eat. This proved far from enough to feed us all. The reason we had survived so long was the mud. The mud in the valley decomposed the buried bodies, but it had no effect on metal. We lived by robbing the graves.

Whenever it rained, we would go into the valley. We would pray to its spirit, ask forgiveness, and then burrow into the hot, supple mud headfirst. We would paddle through searching for rings, bracelets, necklaces, and money pouches bound to the dead. We could see the shine of gold and gemstones through the mud. I had thought that everyone could see that.

Even our backwoods mountain had two or three settlements on it. But my family never talked with the people who lived there. We were outcasts. The village children even threw stones at me. My mother had married Father after he tricked her; after the birth of my younger sister, she left us and ran away. The mother of my two older half-sisters may have been tricked too, but she had died.

I had thought that everyone despised my family because we robbed graves. But that wasn't the only reason. I later learned that we were descended from a union between a human and a ghost. I wondered how that made us different from other people, exactly.

In recent years, no matter how much we searched the mud, we had found nothing. Our family must have retrieved all the precious items from the swamp over time. For several years, Father had given up searching altogether.

"Why did you dig in the mud?" Stonebird asked me now, determined to know more.

"To find gold," I muttered.

"As I thought. Can you swim?"

I shook my head. I had burrowed into the mud headfirst, but at its deepest it came to my chest. I had never had to swim. The current in the river near our house had run too swiftly for swimming. Even my brother had never swum.

"I'll need you to swim," Stonebird said. She stood before me now.

I looked at her face for the first time. She had hard eyes; the irises shone a pale blue. Her long, silver, unkempt hair glinted like gold in the light. She seemed younger than the mother I vaguely remembered. Stonebird's lips were not painted, but nonetheless bright red. She wore a billowing black dress with long sleeves, despite the summer heat.

"Come." She took my hand and made for the exit.

We walked onto a terrace covered in bird droppings. The loud water birds must be asleep somewhere, I thought. Their still-soft droppings squished beneath my feet. As I frowned at the sensation, something covered my face. Stonebird was removing my dress of hempen cloth. No sooner had she stripped me to my underwear than she flung me from the terrace into the lake. A good distance separated the terrace and the water. For a moment, though I knew I was falling, I saw a glow and realized it came from the lights of the capital. Then, plunged into pitch-black water, I began to drown. Stonebird flew down on her broom and pulled me out.

I quickly learned to swim after that.

Every day, Stonebird flung me into the lake. When I would drink water, choke, and begin to drown, she would fly down on her broom and retrieve me. My wet, bare feet soon wore a path across the filthy terrace as I trudged back to the mansion. Stonebird watched me from the terrace each day as I sputtered, so the birds no longer lit there.

Though it was summer, my body grew cold from being in the water first thing every morning. I would warm up in front of the stoves. One of them was always heating a pot of stew, bubbling with meat and vegetables. Did Stonebird cook? I never saw her prepare anything, but the stew was delicious. Every day, it appeared at a different stove, and it tasted different too.

Around the time I began to swim for real, I grew taller and started to fill out. As my father had promised, I was finally well fed.

Once I could swim, I easily learned to dive. The lake did not seem to have clear places; wherever I dove, the water was cloudy. The murk billowed up from the lake bed, spiraling with increasing force to the surface.

One day, Stonebird threw a golden goblet from the terrace. I found it and brought it up. She threw in a gold ring. I counted to twenty before diving but still found it. She threw in a small, transparent stone. I knew it was a diamond; besides gold, I had found jewels in the mud of the valley. When we found a diamond, however small, our whole family had eaten for six months. I counted to fifty before diving for this one. The dark lake bed oozed a murky sludge. Through it, I spotted the diamond.

"Just as I thought," Stonebird said with a satisfied nod.

"There's something I want you to search for, starting tomorrow."

It went without saying that I would search the bottom of the lake.

"There's a pearl," she said.

I knew what a pearl was. There had been pearls in the valley too.

"You found a diamond," Stonebird said. "You can definitely find the pearl."

I guessed the pearl would be about as big as the diamond Stonebird had tossed in the lake, which was the size of the tip of my thumb.

But Stonebird made a circle with the thumbs and forefingers of both hands, using them to frame the moon that rose over the terrace. "It should be about this size," she told me.

The moon that night was full and appeared large. It fit exactly inside the circle Stonebird had formed with her fingers. So, the pearl was that big. Well, I thought, large objects are easier to find than small ones.

Once I learned to swim, I found my new life simple. The water was cold, but Stonebird's stew put lots of padding on my body.

I had only to dive for the pearl. I had no worries. I had confidence that I would find it one day. Finding it became my goal as well as Stonebird's. I wished to know why she wanted the pearl, but I soon forgot about that. Every day I dove until I was exhausted, wolfed down my stew, and slept like the mud itself.

The water grew colder and stung my body, and the number of snowy days increased. Still, I dove every day. On particularly cold days, Stonebird would pull me from the water early.

When that happened and I had energy to spare, it took time to fall asleep. On the nights when I lay awake, I mulled over Stonebird and her home.

Stonebird's mansion, which I could see when floating in the lake, was large. The small room where I slept and the hall with the stoves, and the terrace to which it led, made up the north part. That was the only part of the house that I had explored, but it was less than half. The entire mansion had sheer walls that rose straight up from the ground, with no stairways leading to them. Stonebird must always come and go by broom, I thought. No one who approached by boat would be able to enter. Since I had come here, I had not sensed another person's presence. Then again, if someone had come at night, I might not have known.

Apparently, Stonebird lived in the side of the house opposite mine. It had a larger terrace. *What was the south side like?* I wondered. I wanted to take a look.

Stonebird believed that I would find the pearl, so though she did not treat me well exactly, neither did she push me too far or too roughly. I had been with her for six months. She didn't pay me close attention, just as she rarely noticed the birds who circled overhead. But she noticed whether I stayed healthy enough to use my arms and legs to seek the pearl. Apparently, she saw me as a valuable tool. When she pulled me from the water onto her broom, she would simply ask, "Warm now?" and say nothing further. I, for my part, only nodded. Aside from the way she flew on a broom, Stonebird sometimes seemed just like a normal human.

Snow had been falling since the day before. By late afternoon, I could not see even a short distance through the snow. The lake began to freeze.

The next morning, when I stepped onto the terrace, the blizzard—far from stopping—had grown denser. Still, Stonebird stood with her broom waiting for me. I assumed that today, like every day, I would dive.

But that was not the case. "Today you will rest," Stonebird told me. "This blizzard shows no signs of letting up. And today is New Year's Eve."

She placed a small, hard object in my palm and closed my fingers around it. Then she mounted her broom and took off from the terrace. I thought she might head to the terrace on the opposite side of the house, as usual, but today she flew in a different direction, and I soon lost sight of her. When she didn't reappear, I understood that she must have gone somewhere and would be out for a good while.

The hall was almost hot inside. The object Stonebird had given me stuck to my now-sweaty hand. When I sniffed it, it smelled like ripe fruit. Evidently, it was food. When I licked it, it tasted sweet. I had never encountered sugar before. Today was New Year's Eve, and Stonebird had given me a gift, so New Year's Eve must be special, I thought. Back home, we had done nothing more than sweep our entrance clean for the New Year, which seemed just like any other day. Where had Stonebird gone? I had heard that in the capital, people stayed awake all night to welcome the New Year. I wondered if that was what she planned to do.

She might stay away till tomorrow, I thought. I had no reason to think this, but the idea stuck in my head. And I wished to see the south side of the mansion. For several days, I had dived less than normal. Because I had rested, I had energy to spare.

I walked to the terrace and searched for a way around the house. I could see snow blown by the wind, drifting on the lake's surface. Frozen. I might be able to walk on it. But the distance between the terrace and the lake seemed too long, given that the surface was solid. As I looked down, I noticed that knobs of ice had appeared on the outside walls of the mansion. Snow had stuck to droppings from the birds and frozen. Perhaps these could serve as handholds. I extended my hand to some and touched them. Several fell off right away, but others stayed even when I pressed down hard.

I began to climb down the wall using the knobs as handholds and footholds. Several times I lost my balance, but I didn't fall. When I reached the lake's surface, the ice held fast. It had solidified quickly. I walked around the mansion to the south side, and then I used the knobs again to shimmy up the wall.

The south terrace was larger than mine, but the hall inside the doorless doorway was smaller. In that hall I saw a stairway leading up and another leading down. I headed up.

I found a large room. It too had a stove with a bird sculpture on top, its wings enfolding it. But I saw only one stove, and it was two heads taller than me. The long-necked bird on the stove rested its head at the center of the stove's top. Its eyes were closed. Seeing this, I felt relief. A few embers glowed in the stove; because of them, the room still felt warm. The embers slightly lit the room as well.

Carpets had been spread here and there, and thick cloths hung on the wall. The cloths seemed to have designs on them. I had never touched floors or walls covered in textiles. Even when the smooth floors of this mansion grew cold, I liked them. I had assumed from her name that Stonebird herself liked stone. I had never walked with soft carpet beneath my feet.

Several tables stood at the center of the room, like islands in a lake. One table held grasses and dried insects, stone jars, and a mortar and pestle. One type of grass stank. I knew it must be medicine. I also saw items I did not recognize: stacks of square boxes covered in leather. I did not know then what books were, and besides, I could not read. Another small table held figurines of stone set in lines. That table had two chairs with it. I pictured how my father and older brother had spent evenings facing each other, moving pebbles around. I thought that Stonebird's figurines must be a game. Who was her opponent? I looked about. For the first time, I realized that someone else besides Stonebird and me might dwell in the house. Still, I didn't sense another presence.

Another table held nothing. The chair there was covered with so many animal furs that my body would have sunk right into them. A soft blanket covered a bed several times the size of mine.

Having circled the room once, I came back in front of the stove. A final table held a tapestry frame. Inside the wooden frame stretched a cloth, and next to the chair sat boxes with thread in them. Was Stonebird embroidering something? My eyes had grown used to the dark, but I still could not make out the detailed stitching. I sat in the chair and brought my face close. At that moment, an ember in the stove shifted, and a tongue of flame the size of my palm floated into the air. My heart pounded. Amazingly, I didn't scream. The flame floated right to the tapestry frame. Thinking that it might burn the embroidered cloth, I panicked, but the flame merely floated beside the tapestry and illuminated it.

On the tapestry, I saw many people embroidered in such detail that they looked almost alive. They seemed to be of high status, wearing lavish clothes. They looked like rich people I had seen in the markets. The ladies sparkled with jewels. A man wearing a crown and red cape sat in a shining, gold chair at the center. *He must be the king,* I thought. In front of the king, a young man with silver hair knelt on one knee with his head bowed. Flames flickered in lamps mounted on the walls, and the windows to the left and right of the king showed a black sky. Nighttime.

Excitement filled me. Everything here seemed rare, beautiful, and new. It felt mysterious and strange, and in my ignorance I could barely comprehend it. I saw quite suddenly that the world held fascinating things. I needed to see more of them. That was my one thought.

At the same time, I began to worry about what would happen if I found the pearl. Until now, I had been content to dive in the lake, eating until I was full and staying alive. I had not, until this moment, thought of my future. Suddenly, a wish for freedom took root in my heart.

Chapter Eight

"The Moon Is on the Left"

PART TWO

When I returned to Stonebird's hall and looked outside, the blizzard had worsened.

I descended the lower stairwell. The flame from the tapestry frame moved ahead of me, like a faithful pet.

At the bottom of the steps that led down from the hall, I saw a corridor with three doors on each side. The thick wooden doors had large locks. Iron bars covered small windows in the doors. A dungeon! I stopped. The flame moved on down the corridor, but I stood stock still, my breathing heavy. I sensed a presence.

Someone lived here. Drawing a deep breath, I stepped forward.

The windows were high on the doors. I stood on my tiptoes, pressed against one door, and peered inside. The flame floated above the window for me.

The first cell on each side of the hallway was empty, but the middle cell on the right was occupied. The person lay sleeping under a blanket in a bed pushed against the wall. I saw a child-like, thin body with white hair. I couldn't see the person's face, which was toward the wall. The cell had a small stove. It must have been lit, because the cell was dimly visible. As I expected, the stove had a sculpture of a bird. From where I stood, I couldn't see if its eyes were open or closed.

"Who are you?" I found my voice. "Why are you kept here?"

The voice that answered me came from somewhere else.

"Who's there?" It came from the next cell.

As I turned, the flame moved to float above the small window in the next door. I pressed myself to it and looked inside.

A woman sat on a bed with her head tilted, as though listening carefully. As I peered in, her golden hair moved as she raised her face. Her pale features looked worn, but her voice had traces of youth in it.

"Tell me, who's there?" She faced the door. The light was dim, but she should have seen me. Yet her eyes looked slightly to the side.

"You're not Stonebird, are you?" She stood slowly. "I heard no footsteps. Are you barefoot? Ah, you must be the child who's diving in the lake these days."

She held both hands before her and walked to the door.

"Is Stonebird away? That's odd. Oh, it's New Year's Eve! Stonebird always goes off on New Year's Eve."

She felt for the door with her hands, then gripped the bars of the window and faced me through them. Her hands were white, nearly transparent; she must have been shut in there away from the sun for a long time. But her fingernails were black like mine. I was curious about this, but I was more concerned with other things.

"Your eyes—can you not see?" I asked.

She nodded in answer. "If I could see, I would still be diving, like you. I grew unable to dive, which is why I am locked in here."

I could not speak. I had thought I was the only person who could find Stonebird's pearl. She had said so when she talked to me—or at least I thought she had. Now I felt betrayed.

"There were several people before and after me, as well. All of them died," the woman continued. "Another failed diver is in the cell next to me. Stonebird takes that prisoner upstairs sometimes. She seems attached to him somehow."

She meant the prisoner with white hair. I nodded to show I understood, and then remembered that the woman couldn't see me. I spoke: "I saw someone sleeping on a bed."

I shivered. "Is this where I will end up, too?" My voice caught. Was this my future?

She sensed my apprehension.

"What are you doing hanging about like this? While Stonebird's gone, you should run! If it's December 31, the lake will be frozen. Just like land."

I began to flee before she could finish. She was right. I should have escaped long before this!

"Stop!"

I heard another voice. I'm amazed I heard it. It was low, but it reached my ears. It was the voice of the man on the bed.

"The lake never freezes all the way across!" he warned. "At some point, you'll drop into the water. No matter how used to diving you are, it won't help you now. With no Stonebird to pull you out, you will drown!"

I didn't know which of them to believe.

"Why are you stopping her? Dying would be better than this!" The woman gripped the iron bars and began to laugh. Her voice ricocheted from the ceiling and walls of the dungeon.

Appalled, I stood in the passageway.

"It would be better for you to die!" she went on. "Better than living here, like me. For years! I can't tell you how tired I am!" She stopped laughing and began to cry.

"Go back," the man directed me. "But at some point, escape."

He was telling me to run away, just not right now. I nodded and prepared to go.

"You know something!" The woman accused the man. "It's been ages since I've heard your voice. No matter how often I call out to you, you never answer! What is your relationship to Stonebird? Why does she take you upstairs sometimes? Is she toying with you? Why does she call you Prince? The way she treats you—it's odd.

"And what does she plan for that pearl? Where does she go on New Year's Eve? You know! I'm certain you know! Tell me! Talk! Since you keep ignoring me, I might as well be alone down here!"

The woman both cried and shouted now. She raged at her neighbor in this dungeon, a man who would not speak with her. She must already have resigned herself to the fact that she would never leave.

"Go! Quickly!" Despite the woman's outburst, the man's voice was clear.

I raced up the steps. The floating flame, which had helped me in the dungeon, went on ahead as if its errand were done.

Then I heard a voice on the terrace. "I wish she'd pipe down."

Stonebird was back. She must have heard the woman's voice from outside. I would run right into her! I hurried in the direction the light had gone.

"Quiet!" I heard Stonebird yell. Then, "Come, my dear. It's ready at last. I want to show you." She sounded sickly sweet now. She had not come back alone. Her voice came from behind me, but she didn't descend to the dungeon.

I followed the flame to escape the voice. The flame returned to its place in the upstairs stove, in the carpeted room. I didn't realize it, but the eyes of the bird carved into that stove were open. I went to the stove, as if pulled by the light. The stove was so large that even while standing, I could hide behind it. But just when I thought I was safe, the flames expanded.

How foolish I had been! But there was no time to think of that. I dodged the flames, plastering myself to the soot-blackened wall near the stove.

"Mother, put out the fire, will you? I'm hot."

I heard a young man's voice. Someone who called Stonebird "Mother." *She has a son?*

At the man's words, the fire in the stove shrank as if doused by water. Then, a small flame jumped out again. The flame floated in the air as before.

Stonebird sat at the tapestry frame, and her son stood beside her. The flame from the stove now illuminated the two of them. Their hair was the same color: silver, but glinting gold.

"Look here, do you see? It's finished at last. I have only to add the pearl."

"This spell has taken forever, Mother," Stonebird's son said, lit by the floating flame.

I had never seen a man so handsome. He looked pure, innocent—the kind of person anyone would love.

"This spell had to be cast with one pass of the needle, then another, and another," Stonebird explained to him. "It took time, but there was no other way."

"You're amazing, Mother." Stonebird's son was buttering her up now.

"The prince in the coronation scene is you," Stonebird told him. Her hand caressed his cheek.

She had embroidered a king's coronation. And in the scene, the man being crowned was on bended knee—and he resembled Stonebird's son. It was, in fact, his very self.

"I'm sick of living in this form," her son whined.

I didn't know what he meant as he seemed a beautiful, well-proportioned man.

"You must wait," Stonebird said. "It won't do for this plan to fail. The spell calls for the real prince of the land to disappear, and then reappear at the coronation when he is twenty years old. The one who will appear is, of course, not him, but you. For this, I have cast the spell for twenty years. Nothing I could do would alter time itself." She seemed to regret this.

"It's been twenty years," he said. "Finally. What's the prince up to these days?"

"He's no use to me anymore, so I've locked him up downstairs. Sometimes I have him play chess with me, but he's barely more than a shadow now."

"You're good at chess, aren't you, Mother?"

"Not bad," she agreed. "He's a fine strategist, though." She shook her head in wonder.

"Well, you raised him, right?" the son said.

"So I did. That must be why!" she answered. The two of them laughed.

"The day I add the moon to the tapestry will be the day of the coronation," Stonebird said seriously. "That day, you will become king."

"Have you found it yet?" the son asked. "Do you think it's really out in the lake?"

"I know it's there. In my grandmother's generation, the royal family fled the war-torn capital and sought refuge in this mansion. They hoped my grandmother's magic would save them, but their enemies caught up to them and sank their boat. The pearl belonged to the queen who died in that boat. It holds heartache. That's precisely why I involved it in this spell. I have found the other jewels. Surely, it won't be long until I have the pearl.

"We're searching the east side now. That's the only part left. This child I have will surely find it. She's Polonia, you know."

"You've said that before, Mother," the son complained.

They were talking of me. And of how the pearl would complete the tapestry as the moon. By adding the moon,

Stonebird would finish her spell. A coronation would take place. And her son would become king. I failed to understand one detail: what did Polonia mean?

"When we find the moon, I will place it on the left."

"The moon on the left of the throne—the magic moon. Its light will make me visible," Stonebird's son said. "No more melting into darkness."

"That's right, and thanks to the moon you really will return to life. You will be crowned king of the country that killed you. You'll take revenge for every bit of your suffering, Son! I know you will."

"Now then, I'd better take you back," said Stonebird. "How I love New Year's Eve! The magic protecting the castle weakens, and I can see you!"

Stonebird embraced her son.

Killed? Return to life? Melt into darkness? I grew confused all over again.

"Do I have to go back?" the son sighed.

"Forgive me. I know it's unpleasant under that unbefitting gravestone, with all the ghosts about. Wait a bit more. When you're king, all will be as you wish. You can fill this land with hatred and fighting, just as you like!"

Stonebird said he dwelled with ghosts. Was he a spirit of the dead? He looked normal.

"You're right, Mother. I can't wait!" The son's voice sounded supremely satisfied. Flattened against the wall behind the stove, I felt myself shiver.

The floating flame returned to the stove. Stonebird's footsteps grew faint. She had taken her son away.

I trembled now. If I found the pearl, horrid things would happen! The world would fill with hate. I knew nothing of war, but I feared people dying. My father, despite being a grave minder—or perhaps because of it— had found death frightening. He had clung to life so fiercely that he sold his children rather than face death. I had seen his fear, so I too feared death. And now I knew that hundreds, perhaps thousands, of people could die. How could I let myself be part of that?

Should I just not find the pearl? I wondered. If I failed to find it, Stonebird would buy a new child and have her search in my place. I knew now that it didn't matter who searched the lake. I had felt important and believed Stonebird when she said, "You're the one." I had tried to be useful to her because of that, even though she had bought me. I had been so wrong. Many others had dived—there was nothing special about me. And in the end, I would be shut up in the dungeon. I would be jailed there, crying and wailing like the woman I'd met. I didn't want that. I wanted to escape. But I didn't know how.

Before me, the embers glowed brightly. I recalled how earlier, I had worried that the floating flame would singe the tapestry. If I stirred the embers, the flames would grow. I could burn the tapestry. What would happen if I did? Stonebird's spell would surely change somehow. I would no longer have to dive for the pearl.

There. I would do it. The whole room would burn. They would never know I was responsible. I would take care that the flames didn't spread downstairs.

I crept from behind the stove. I got ready to spread the fire.

"Aha!"

Someone seized my collar. Stonebird. She hadn't taken her son back after all.

"Hiding from me, were you?" She held me in the air with one hand and peered at my face. Then she laughed as though it were funny. Her eyes darted to the ash near the stove. I followed her gaze. My footprints showed clearly in the ash. And the eyes of the stone bird were open.

"Well, look what got stuck by the stove!" Stonebird's son poked me with his index finger.

"Let me go!" I bit the son's finger like a frightened kitten.

"Say, she can see me. Even in this dim light. A Polonia, huh?" Shaking his sore finger, the son smiled ruefully.

I had no time to process his words.

"Why couldn't you simply stay in your room? I never thought you'd get up to mischief." Stonebird clicked her tongue. "Well, you heard everything. I can't use you anymore. Come!"

She began to drag me. Her command had been for the fire in the stove, because again, a flame flew out and lit the way.

"No! NO! I won't go to that awful place!" I cried.

I had learned, moments before in this room, that the world held wonders I had never seen. I had begun to look forward to leaving this prison someday, and to seeing the world for myself. Now I faced a real dungeon. My heart broke. Tears flooded my face.

"So you've had a look downstairs."

Stonebird dragged me down the stairwell. My bottom smacked into the stairs, but the dungeon scared me more than any pain.

"Mother, what about the pearl? This girl is the one, right? The Polonia? Even you will have a hard time finding someone to replace her."

Stonebird's son followed us.

"I'll figure it out. The pearl is the only object left," Stonebird answered. "I'll buy another child. I'll buy dozens more."

She opened the door to a cell with one hand, and prepared to fling me in.

"Is the spell complete?" I heard the voice of the man in his cell nearby.

"All she needs is the moon," I answered. "Then the coronation will happen! And her ghost son will become king!"

I was shouting. Stonebird slapped my cheek. "What are you talking about?"

I slammed into a wall.

"Say, Prince, it's you! Still alive, huh?" the son asked. "Just like my mother said. I can barely see you now."

The son peered into the man's window and smiled. He had called the man in the cell Prince.

"Listen. Listen to me." For the first time, the man with white hair showed his face at the window. Pure skin and bones. They'd said he was now twenty, the same age Stonebird's son was when he died, but he looked decades older, this man who was the real prince of the land.

"I know where you can find the pearl," he said.

"You do?" Stonebird exclaimed.

"I discovered it, and I've been hiding it. No one can find it now."

"MOTHER!" Stonebird's son implored her to do something.

"He's found it, has he?" Stonebird said. "If it's true, then I'm in a bind, aren't I?"

"You are."

"Here I tried to keep my plan secret, to prevent something like this," Stonebird said, her face disappointed.

"It's because you made him dive like the others! What'll you do now?" the son demanded, grabbing Stonebird's cloak like a spoiled child.

"Only a child's eyes can see through the lake's murky depths. And Polonia children can see even better. But there aren't many Polonias, Son. And this lake is large. My one choice was to get many children to dive, so I made him dive too. He discovered the pearl long ago, it seems . . . Prince, you duped me completely," Stonebird finished.

She glanced at me again. She had once more said *Polonia*.

I heard someone gasp. The woman prisoner threw her body against her door and looked out with her sightless eyes. She opened her mouth as though to speak, but only stood there, gripping the bars in her window.

"Even a child knows when he's found something precious," the prince continued. "You're the fool, Stonebird, for thinking I would give it to you."

"How dare you! How many children do you think I brought here? Are you saying that it was all a waste?" Stonebird stomped a foot angrily. "So what do you want from me?" she asked, glaring at the prince's window.

"I'll give you the pearl. In exchange, you let us out of here. All three of us."

"Aaaah!" The woman prisoner called, unable to contain herself.

"How can we?" Stonebird's son muttered.

"We have no choice," Stonebird reminded him.

"If you release them and people learn this man is the prince, what happens to me?" her son raised his voice.

"The spell is complete," Stonebird reassured him. "All we need now is the pearl. At any cost. The prince who comes back to life for the coronation will need to be a strong, handsome youth. Everyone will see that you are the man who fits that description! If the prince went to the castle today and shouted that he was the long-lost heir to the throne, who would believe him? People would think him mad—they might even toss him into the castle dungeon. Plus, he has lived in this mansion since the day after his birth. He doesn't even know the way to the castle!"

"I took good care of him. He had food. He had a warm place to sleep. If he leaves, what can he do? It'll be all he can manage to stay alive." Stonebird sneered.

As Stonebird said, it seemed impossible for the prince to return to the castle. Still, I thrilled at the thought that he might not be kept here anymore.

"Well, you should return," Stonebird told her son. "Once the spell takes effect, you will have to be in the castle for it to work. I'll take you to the graveyard."

Stonebird and her son climbed the steps.

"Will you let us out?" the prince called after her.

"Yes. When I come back, I'll have you give me the pearl," Stonebird replied. "On the first day of the new year, you'll live outside this mansion for the first time. Looking forward to it?" Cackling, she vanished up the steps.

I remained in the corridor, never locked into my cell. They had forgotten about me.

The prince peered out of his window.

"Where's the pearl?" I asked him, unthinking.

The prince brought his finger to his lips to quiet me. Then he mouthed, "I don't know."

"What?!" I almost screamed, and then quickly covered my mouth with both hands.

"Are they gone?" he mouthed next, pointing up the stairs with his finger. He wanted to make sure Stonebird had taken her son away. I nodded and ran up the steps.

I sat on the top step and looked toward the terrace. Before long, I heard Stonebird speak again.

"It was a good New Year's Eve, wasn't it?" she said. "We'll have the pearl soon! It's just a waiting game now. The castle will soon be ours."

"I'm sick of being a ghost," her son answered. "The coronation can't come soon enough."

The two of them
flew on the broom
into the falling snow.
I was determined not
to be tricked this time.
I watched intently as they
disappeared in the blizzard.

"She took her son back," I said to the
prince as I rushed down the stairs. "I wonder
where they went."

"They went to the castle," he answered. "Many
years ago, Stonebird's son tried to seize the castle in
a takeover and failed. He was captured and executed.
Now he's a ghost that haunts the execution ground.
She brings him here every New Year's Eve."

"So he is a ghost?" I cried. "He looks like a normal
person!"

"Because of his mother's magic, he now becomes
visible when in direct light," the prince said. "When I
was a child, he was nothing more than a shadow. When
the spell takes hold, he really will return to life."

I began to nod in response. Then, I realized I had
been able to see the son without light. I had bit his
finger. I began to mention this, but then the prince
spoke again.

"More importantly, now's our chance. Where could
that pearl be?"

I thought he was addressing me. I shook my head
and began to say I didn't know.

But the woman answered. "Until now, the large jewels have either been snared in water plants in the north part of the lake, or sunken in fish nests in the southeast. Stonebird believes that large jewels don't move around in the currents, but she could be wrong."

"The east side is the only place that's never been searched," continued the prince. "So Stonebird thinks the pearl is on the east side. But the east side is the path for water from the west side. The current is swift, so there aren't many fish and no water plants can grow. The lake bed is smooth there. There's nothing for jewels to get caught in.

"Stonebird began her search in the north part of the lake," he went on. "When I was a child, I dove there. The pearl may well have washed through the northeast part. Have you seen anything it might get tangled in?"

The prince was addressing me this time. Suddenly I couldn't speak.

"Don't be afraid. We are not actually enemies."

"We've been tricking Stonebird so she wouldn't pay attention to us. If she knew that we had discussions, she would have separated us."

The prince and the woman took turns speaking.

"As I said before," the prince went on, "I don't know where the pearl is. As a child, I believed Stonebird was my mother. I dove in the lake and searched for jewels for her, like a good boy."

His face twisted in sadness. He'd been raised in this place since the day after his birth. He couldn't help but think of Stonebird as his mother back then. And Stonebird, for her part, had used his feelings to benefit herself. I could never forgive her.

"The woman I thought of as Mother shut me into this dungeon," the prince continued. "Even if she treated me horribly, I wanted to believe she was my mother. When I realized this wasn't the truth, my hair turned white in a single day."

For the prince, having his royal status taken away must have been far less troubling than having who he thought of as his mother betray him.

"This is our last chance to escape this place. Based on our experiences and those of others, we might be able to solve this," the prince said.

"What do you think?" he asked me. "Do you have ideas as to where the pearl might be?"

Stonebird was correct: this prince was a strategist.

I remembered the north end of the lake bed. I had seen it only from far away while diving else-where, but through the murk, something had struck me as strange.

"The boul-ders beneath the cliffs on the north end. Something could be there," I said. "But—"

I fell silent.

We heard Stonebird's footsteps on the stairway.

The story in *Daisy* ended here.

CHAPTER NINE

Dead Ends

I looked up from *Daisy* to find it had gotten dark outside. In the enclosed porch at Mrs. Andō's, the ceiling light had been switched on. A glass of barley tea sat next to me with a plate of mizu yōkan.

"Was the story interesting?" Mrs. Andō asked. She wiped her hands on her apron as she watched me.

"It was. I—I'm sorry, what time is it?"

How long had I been sitting there?

"It's past seven. Why don't you have supper before you go? I was about to call your mother."

Mrs. Andō must get lonely eating supper alone, I thought. I would have stayed, but I worried that if I did, I would tell her about Akari—that is, about Saori.

As I got up, I asked Mrs. Andō, "May I please borrow the magazines? I'll take good care of them, I promise. I'd like to show the story to a friend."

Akari deserved to read "The Moon Is on the Left," even if it was unfinished. And there was no way I could bring her here.

Mrs. Andō thought for a moment. "Sure, that would be fine," she replied. "You were so absorbed in reading it! I think stories would rather be read than collecting dust on a shelf, don't you?" She put the issues of *Daisy* in a shopping bag and handed it to me.

"I'll take good care of them," I said. "As soon as I can make a copy, I'll return them." I headed out and loaded the shopping bag into my bicycle basket.

As I pedaled home, I broke into a sweat. Mrs. Andō's air conditioner had been on full blast. I'd been so into the story, set in a blizzard, that I'd forgotten it was summer.

"And what took you so long, young man? I hope you weren't bothering Mrs. Andō!"

Mom's tone was harsh, but she'd known where I was. She wasn't actually upset.

"I needed something for summer homework."

Such a useful excuse.

"The president of the neighborhood association won't be coming again. Right?"

Mom had hated that. I waved my hand to show it wouldn't happen again.

After supper, I took "The Moon Is on the Left" to the convenience store and copied the entire story. I took the copy to Akari's house.

She was there.

"I can't believe it, Kazu! How wonderful! I'm amazed you found this, even if it doesn't have the ending. I've so wanted to read it again . . . thank you, thank you!"

Akari clasped her hands to her chest again and hopped around.

I wanted to tell her she was holding a copy made from her own issues of *Daisy*, but I kept my mouth shut.

I went home and fired up Uncle Junichi's computer. I got my sister to show me how to look up books online. Akari had said the bookstores didn't stock "The Moon Is on the Left," and sure enough, it got no hits. The story must not have been finished. I felt let down. I wanted to know what would happen to Adi.

I got no results for the author Mia Lee, either. Where was she from? Was she Chinese? Maybe the whole story was out in Chinese! But my sister didn't know how to search for that.

I gave up and went to sleep. Stumped yet again. Nothing new.

The next day at radio exercises, I looked around for Akari. I spotted her and felt relieved. But she looked less cheerful than the night before. Her eyes were puffy. *She's been crying*, I thought.

She jogged up to where I stood. "Thank you so much again!" she said. "The story was every bit as good as I remembered!" I realized that she must not have cried; she had only stayed up late reading "The Moon Is on the Left," through the last page we had.

"I used to get so excited to read the next installment of that story every month . . . I would wait so impatiently for the next issue. I never forgot it."

Akari knew that I knew who she was now, so she talked about her old life easily.

"I read the story too," I told her. "I even looked it up online, but I couldn't find anything by searching for the title or author. I wonder if she finished it? I wonder if she's from China?"

"She's probably not from abroad—"

"But, Mia Lee!"

"If the story had come from abroad, wouldn't they give a translator's name?"

She was right.

"Well, maybe it was written in Japanese," I said.

"True—people from outside Japan sometimes write in Japanese," she agreed.

"Or maybe a Japanese writer used a pen name," I added.

"Well, look who's here!" Yūsuke said as he ran up and clapped me on the shoulders. He was all worked up. He looked from me to Akari and back again meaningfully.

"Hmm . . ." I started to say.

"We were talking about a serialized story in an old magazine!" Akari broke in. "Kazu read it too!"

"Whoah. Kazu, you read something?" Yūsuke opened his eyes wide.

I nodded vaguely, and the music for radio exercises began.

Akari skipped off to where the girls were.

"Kazu, something's up with you. Do you like Akari?" Yūsuke looked as though he couldn't fathom another explanation.

"We read the same story, that's all. She just told you!" I said.

"Is it really that good?"

"Yeah, and it has no ending. So it's hard to stop thinking about it."

He and I talked while doing our exercises halfheartedly.

"What do you mean, there's no ending?" he asked.

"It was published in a monthly magazine, but we don't have all the issues," I said. "It's from forty years ago, so it's hard to track down."

"Forty years ago? That's ancient history!" Yūsuke swung around. "Are you really OK?"

"Of course I am, you idiot!" As I said that, I realized that for three days, I had learned things but had made tons of mistakes. I was disappointed in myself. Maybe that meant I was growing up. Yūsuke may have picked up on that. I sighed.

When radio exercises ended, he and I headed home. Akari caught up with us.

"Kazu, you want to go to the beach tomorrow?" Yūsuke was asking me. "We're setting up a stand at Mitohama."

Yūsuke's family doesn't sell merchandise only at their store. They sometimes set up shop in large hospitals, factories, and civic offices in the mountains. Long ago, folks in these isolated areas appreciated having merchants come to them. Even now, when people have cars and shop in town, Yūsuke's family has clients at a cannery in Mitohama, on the coast about two and a half hours from Minami Ōdori. Since preschool, I've ridden there with them and swum in the sea with Yūsuke. His dad drives us to the beach and hangs out with us, which his job doesn't usually let him do. He likes taking his son for a treat, but since he can't swim, he never ventures into the water himself. If anything, he sunbathes. He says that a summertime tan is stylish.

"Yeah, the beach sounds good," I said to Yūsuke. I turned to Akari. "Akari, you want to come?"

"Really? Wow! I'd love to!" Akari answered, hopping in her usual way.

Yūsuke looked at me questioningly. Confused or not, he would never mistreat a future customer.

"Sure, come with us!" he said, nodding as if he'd never been mystified.

"I'll have to get my mom to buy me a swimsuit," Akari said. "I'll need a floaty, because I can't swim. I'll pack a lunch . . ." She counted her to-dos on her fingers.

"Don't worry about bringing a lunch," Yūsuke said. "It's hot, so it'll spoil. We'll buy *yakisoba* at the beach!" As usual, Yūsuke was all about the fried noodles. His excitement was contagious.

"I can't wait! I'll see you two tomorrow!" Akari was so thrilled she could barely contain herself. She ran past us toward home.

"Come to our store's parking lot tomorrow at seven!" Yūsuke called to her.

"You'll need flip-flops! And sunscreen!" I yelled.

She had never been to the seashore. I worried for her.

"OK!" she called, her red baubles bobbing.

Her excitement almost made me cry. She would be seeing the ocean for the first time, ever. Yet the second she put her toes in the surf might be when she would fade away. I had to beg Ms. Minakami again. I made up my mind then and there.

"Did you, um, want to go to the beach with Akari?" Yūsuke asked me. He stopped in front of his store.

"Sorry, I invited her without asking you. It's just that she was with us," I apologized.

"It's OK. It's weird, though, 'cause I thought for sure you and Ami would pair up."

"What do you mean? I don't like Akari that way!"

"Then what's up with you two?" he asked.

"We were talking. I mean, we read the same story."

"Oh, right. The one with no ending."

"Yeah, and I want to get the ending for her to rea—I mean for me, to read," I corrected myself.

"Why isn't there an ending? Did the magazine go out of print?" Yūsuke asked.

"I don't know," I answered. "It was a long time ago."

"Did you ask the publisher?" he asked casually.

"You're right! The publisher!" I shouted. "That's who I should ask." Yūsuke was a genius.

"*If* the publisher's still around," he added.

"I'll find out," I said.

"But more importantly, when do we hit the pool?" Yūsuke was ready to move on to a new topic.

"What's a good time?"

"I've got cram school this morning."

"OK. I'll meet you this afternoon," I said. "Let's go to the city pool. I have an errand that way."

I had to return the issues of *Daisy* to Mrs. Andō.

"Sounds good," Yūsuke agreed.

That morning I stayed busy.

At the stroke of eight, I was in the lobby of Minami Heights leaning on the buzzer. It was early, but I couldn't wait. Ms. Minakami didn't answer. Had she overslept? Knowing full well that I would get scolded, I pressed the buzzer again. Finally, the superintendent came over from the entryway, where he had been cleaning.

"If it's Ms. Minakami you're after, she's been away since yesterday."

"Yesterday?"

"She takes overnight trips sometimes. She's doing free trials of assisted-living facilities. She's still so fit that I tell her it's too early, but she insists that she has to investigate her options before she's too old. Anyway, that lady does what she pleases."

"You can say that again," I said. "She's stubborn, and she's mean too!"

"Ah, ha-ha. That's true. But she's sharp. I'd like to grow old that way myself." The super, who looked to be in his seventies, flashed a smile.

"She's *so* bullheaded, though," I replied.

The super threw me a sly glance. "I'll be sure to pass that on, from the little boy who came to see her."

"My name is Kazuhiro Sada!" I told him.

I was sick of the cute-kid treatment.

At nine on the dot, I was phoning K Company, the publisher listed in *Daisy*. As expected, I got a recording: *The number you have dialed . . .*

I was disappointed, but I knew that forty years had passed. Then I called the operator, who gave me the new number for K Company right away.

I called and said I wanted to know about *Daisy*, a discontinued monthly magazine. After several transfers, I was connected to a woman named Ms. Date (pronounced "Dah-tay").

"What can I help you with regarding *Daisy*?"

Ms. Date knew I was a fifth grader, but she spoke as if I were an adult. I appreciated that.

"I'm interested in the story 'The Moon Is on the Left,' which was serialized in *Daisy*," I told her.

"I understand that *Daisy* was the forerunner to our current manga magazine *Chocolat*," Ms. Date said. "During the *Daisy* period, I guess stories were published along with manga. I didn't know that!"

"The six issues I have contain parts one and two of the story, ending with the installment of part two published in December 1972. I can't seem to get the issues after that," I said.

"*Daisy* was published through 1975," Ms. Date told me. "I believe you can still read the rest of that story, but the copies of the magazine that we still have are for record-keeping purposes. We can't sell them to you."

"Really?" I began to groan.

"If you could come to our headquarters, you could have a look," she said.

"But that's in Tokyo, right?" I said.

"Do you live outside of Tokyo, Mr. Sada?"

"Yes, I live in Masuda city," I replied. I forgot to add the prefecture name. I figured she might not understand me, but then she responded:

"Masuda, the 'Little Kyoto,' where cherry blossoms are beautiful every year!" Ms. Date knew that my town attracts tourists from throughout Japan every spring. Our population sometimes swells to three times its normal size during cherry blossom season.

"Since you can't come here, why don't I simply have a copy of the story sent to you?" she offered.

Ms. Date was my hero. I gave her my postal address and even our email.

Then I ran to Akari's house. I wanted to cheer her up with the good news, but nobody was home. She might have gone to buy her swimsuit, I thought. What a day—I kept missing people. I went home and stared at my math drills for school, but then Mom called me.

She had the phone in her hand and an annoyed look on her face.

"It's a Ms. Date, calling from a publisher in Tokyo!" She held out the phone. "What are you up to?" she whispered.

"I told you—summer homework!"

I turned my back to Mom and spoke into the phone.

"I'm glad I caught you!" Ms. Date said. "I took a look at *Daisy*. It's very unfortunate, but the story you were reading seems to stop with the last issue you have. The next one has a message to readers, stating that the story is on hold, due to the author's circumstances."

I felt so disappointed I wanted to collapse on the floor. "Why would the story stop?" I asked.

"I'm afraid I don't know. In the next year's February issue, there are letters from readers saying they look forward to the next installment. Mia Lee seems to have had fans. Mr. Sada, how did you learn about 'The Moon Is on the Left'?"

She seemed mystified, which was reasonable. I was asking about a magazine for girls, after all, from forty years ago.

"Somebody recommended it to me. They said the story was really good—"

"Was it your mother?"

I calculated quickly. If Akari had lived, she would have been older than my mom. "I heard about it from a lady I know," I said.

"You must like to read, Mr. Sada. Is that why she showed it to you?"

Ms. Date had the mistaken impression that I was a book-worm. She told me that she would inform me as soon as she learned anything further about Mia Lee. But I knew that no matter what we learned about the author, the story was still incomplete.

Unable to give up, I headed back to Minami Heights. Ms. Minakami was still away. On the way home, I spotted Akari walking along next to a shopping bag that swung around suspended in the air. I shivered at the creepy sight, even though I knew Invisible Mama was holding the bag. At least Akari hadn't vanished yet.

I headed back to Mrs. Andō's house with Yūsuke and returned the issues of *Daisy*. Then Yūsuke and I went to the pool. It was beginning to feel like summer vacation, finally, but with Akari on my mind, I couldn't enjoy myself.

"Kazu, you seem off," Yūsuke said, looking at me as we sat on the side of the pool.

I'd planned to consult him about Akari, but too much had happened. Now I couldn't say a word. "There's nothing going on," I told him.

I smiled as if to show I meant it, but Yūsuke glared back at me. He could tell I was lying. He's my friend, so even though he never shows up on time, he knows me well.

"Yūsuke! I love you!" I gave him a hug.

"Stop it, you creep!" Yūsuke pushed me. I grabbed him again. We pushed and shoved until we toppled into the water.

That night, I packed for the beach and then sat at the computer.

I had a message from Uncle Junichi. I felt awful telling him I'd lost the statuette.

I see. Well, if you looked for it and it's not there, there's not much we can do. Kimyō Temple is mainly stories that I don't entirely believe myself. Grandpa did say, though, that we should take care of it. It's too bad.

I replied to him:

I'm sorry.

That was all I could write. It was the truth. I'd done something unforgivable. I had ruined Akari's life. I wished I could tell my uncle everything.

There was also a message from Ms. Date of K Company.

I learned a bit about Mia Lee. My former supervisor has retired, but when she first worked here she helped with *Daisy.* She remembers "The Moon Is on the Left."

She wasn't directly in charge of the project, so she doesn't know Mia Lee's real name. However, she's certain Mia Lee was an aspiring manga artist who never quite launched her career. She worked hard, but her illustrations seemed not to appeal to *Daisy* readers. The drawings in "The Moon Is on the Left" are Mia Lee's. People advised her to try illustrating literature instead of manga, so she did.

When I told my former supervisor that someone from Masuda had asked about Mia Lee, she said she was pretty sure Mia Lee was from Masuda herself. She remembers her talking about Little Kyoto.

Daisy was an experimental magazine, and it mainly circulated in large cities. I can only guess, but I wonder if the person who showed you "The Moon Is on the Left" knows Mia Lee.

Ms. Date seemed to mean that I should ask my acquaintance, if I wanted to know more.

I called up Mrs. Andō.

"Did Saori start reading *Daisy* because someone gave her the magazine?" I asked.

"Yes," Mrs. Andō replied. "Your grandfather, Mr. Sada, gave us our first issue. After that, Saori would always ask me to buy the next one, so I ordered it from the bookstore. Since you've been studying your grandpa, I assumed you had found something about it in his old schedule book or diary. Because you came over specifically to read *Daisy*."

YES! I wanted to yell. At last I had a clue. But . . . Grandpa? Would he really have bought a girls' magazine for Saori?

"My grandpa gave it to her?" I asked, sounding startled.

"I was going to mention it yesterday, if we'd had more time," Mrs. Andō said.

That was why she'd invited me to supper.

"Kazuhiro, your grandfather got the magazine from a friend. Actually, the parents of the person who wrote the story gave it to him. He told me he was grateful to receive it, but he only had boys at home, and they were still small and into picture books. He thought Saori might like it. When I saw you reading it yesterday, though, I realized boys could enjoy that story too!"

She laughed a little and we said goodbye.

I went and bugged my dad. "Did Grandpa have a friend whose daughter wanted to be a manga artist?" I asked him.

"Ummm, not that I know of. He knew somebody who wrote haiku, I think."

"How about Grandma's friends?"

"Don't think so. She didn't mingle with artist types."

With that, the conversation ended. I started to head upstairs, but then I remembered Mrs. Andō mentioning

Grandpa's diary. Grandpa had not kept a journal, but he had carried little black notebooks where he wrote down stuff he wanted to remember.

I turned and headed to his room, which was now more like a storage area. My mom kept saying we'd clean it out, but Grandma and Grandpa's clothes and belongings were all still there. By the time I found a cardboard box in the closet, bulging with Grandpa's notebooks, it was after eleven.

Mom came in with a scary face. "Aren't you going to the beach tomorrow?" she said. "You'd better get to sleep, or you'll be crabby tomorrow. I don't want you annoying Yūsuke's dad. Go!"

I pulled out the notebook from 1972 and headed to my room. The issue Akari received had been from July of that year, but it would have been available before the actual month. I scanned Grandpa's sloppy writing. I desperately wanted to figure out who he had seen and where he had gone. But I feared there might be no mention of receiving a girls' magazine. I kept looking. Had he scrawled any names with a connection to Mia Lee? I searched and searched, but at some point, I fell asleep.

CHAPTER TEN

Who Is Mia Lee?

The next morning, I went and did radio exercises. Then I downed my breakfast and headed to Yūsuke's parking lot. Akari and Invisible Mama arrived soon after me.

Akari's mother thanked Yūsuke's family, and me as well. "I hope you have a fun time. Akari was so excited she barely slept last night!"

I was glad not to be the only one low on sleep.

Yūsuke's family vehicle is like a minibus. You can load tons of stuff in it and still seat five or six people. Besides Yūsuke, Akari, and me, our group today included Yūsuke's dad (driving as always), plus a worker I knew from the shop named Ms. Shiraki. Plus—oh no—Yūsuke's grandma, an intimidating lady. I guess that's no surprise since she's the ruler of a kimono empire. She has nerves of steel and gives off a scary aura. She and my mom might as well be different species.

Yūsuke's grandma sat down by Akari and tried one of the hard candies Akari had brought. "This is delicious," she said daintily. But she chewed it ferociously, cracking it between her teeth. She's over eighty, but no one messes with her. She still does a lot at the store and will no doubt live to a ripe old age.

Akari pulled out her copy of "The Moon Is on the Left."

"Yūsuke, you should read this too," she said, handing him the story.

"Oh, is it the story you and Kazu are so into?" Yūsuke flipped through the pages.

I figured he wouldn't read it. Yūsuke reads less than I do. But since I was absorbed in Grandpa's notebook, Yūsuke began to glance at the story. My own reading consisted of names like Yamamoto and Suzuki, but I found no mention of Mia Lee. At some point I dozed off.

"Kazu, we're here."

Yūsuke shook me awake. Yūsuke's grandma was waking Akari.

At the cannery, we pushed tables together in the corner of the employees' cafeteria and arranged merchandise on them. We also set out racks of clothing. (The racks looked like the floating laundry hanger at Akari's house.) I was used to helping with these chores. Akari helped too, commenting in amazement, "Wow, Yūsuke, I didn't know you also sell Western clothes!"

Afterward Yūsuke, his dad, Akari, and I headed to the Mitohama Beach Swimming Area. We had fun. I enjoyed myself because, well, Akari was still there. We all ate fried noodles from the shack on the beach, got shaved ice, sunbathed, and took pictures. I wondered when Akari might vanish from the pictures, but for now, her smile lit up all of them.

"With a special guest among us, we'd better go all out!" Yūsuke's dad announced. He rented beach umbrellas and a small boat that he gave us a ride in. I was as happy for Akari as I was for myself.

A little after three, we packed up at the cannery and headed home. Before he drifted to sleep in the minibus, Yūsuke returned "The Moon Is on the Left" to Akari.

"Did you read it, Yūsuke? Good job!" I messed up his hair.

"I wonder what happens at the end," he said.

"I wish we knew!" Akari replied.

"Um, I bet the lady in the dungeon and Adi are—" Yūsuke started to say.

"Sisters!"

"Exactly!" Yūsuke and Akari were getting all excited.

"I called the publisher, you know," I told them.

"Whoa, way to go, Kazu!" Yūsuke clapped me on the shoulder.

"Ow!" I jumped from my seat. "That hurts!"

"You're sunburned," Akari said. Her nose and shoulders were red like mine.

"Hey, you should cool off after this," I told her. "The pharmacy sells a special lotion for sunburns. You should go buy some. Or stop by my house, and I'll give you my sister's."

Everything was new for Akari, even a sunburn. I didn't want her to be uncomfortable. Yūsuke noticed this and eyed me with a sly grin. I wanted to scream that he had it wrong.

"Apparently Mia Lee is from our town," I said—not to change the subject, of course. Just to share what I'd learned.

"What?" Akari and Yūsuke yelped in surprise.

"My grandpa knew her."

"What?" Akari and Yūsuke sang in unison again.

"I bet if we went to the city museum, somebody there would know her," Yūsuke said.

"Well . . . if she had published a book, maybe. But she stopped writing before the end of this story," I said. "I heard she wanted to be a manga artist but her career never took off."

"Manga, are you serious?" Yūsuke asked.

"She illustrated "The Moon Is on the Left," I told him.

Yūsuke stared at the minibus ceiling, while Akari flipped through the pages again.

"These drawings might have been off-putting," she acknowledged. "They're a little scary."

"They're in silhouette, aren't they?"

As we three flipped through the pages, Yūsuke's grandma coughed loudly. "A-hem."

How could she be hoarse? She had swallowed almost all of Akari's hard candy. Barely left any for us.

"Forty years ago, right? I wonder if she's still alive." Akari spoke in a wistful voice.

"If she were alive, she might be about sixty," I said.

"That's too young," Yūsuke countered.

"But some manga artists start out in their teens," I pointed out.

Yūsuke's grandma coughed again. Akari began digging in her bag for another candy.

"Yeah, your sister's manga books said something about that," Yūsuke said.

"You guys read girls' manga?" Akari asked, surprised.

Yūsuke's grandma coughed a third time.

Akari and I both dug in our bags. Surely one piece of candy was left.

"When are you going to ask me what I might know?" Yūsuke's grandma piped up, glaring at each one of us.

At first, I could barely process what she was saying.

"OH WOW!" The three of us practically screamed.

"Grandma, do you read girls' manga?!" Yūsuke wanted to know.

"Do you know Mia Lee?" I asked.

"I can't believe it! I can't believe it!" Akari looked ready to cross her hands and start hopping again.

"You need someone from this town who knew Kazu's grandpa, right?" Yūsuke's grandma asked. "Use your heads. Kazu's grandpa and I were the same age. I grew up at Takamatsuya, the center of this neighborhood. Who better do you have to ask?" She chuckled. "I've forgotten the name, but I got a copy of the same magazine your grandpa received."

"YOU DID?" We cried out together again. We must have been louder this time, because Yūsuke's dad turned around.

"Eyes on the road!" Yūsuke's grandma commanded.

"So, you don't remember the magazine called *Daisy*, but you remember the author?" I asked, my heart pounding.

"Of course, I do. Mia Lee was ahead of me in school."

Mia Lee was from Masuda, and from this very district! And in her eighties. I began to get a premonition. My jaw dropped.

"The girls in my class knew why she used that pen name," Yūsuke's grandma went on. "When we were young, it was fashionable to take one sound from each character in our names and create a nickname. Silly, isn't it? I was called Tashifu."

"Cool, Grandma. Like a pirate name!" Yūsuke was into it.

"You used one sound from each character in your names, so *Ta* from Taka in Takamatsu," said Akari.

"Right, and the character for *matsu*, pine, can be read *shō*, which includes the sound *shi*," said Yūsuke's grandma. "So *Ta-shi*. And my first name is Tomi, which can be read *fu*. *Ta-shi-fu*.

"I could have made other names, too," Yūsuke's grandma pointed out. "But each of us chose the combination we liked best, and we told our closest friends. Then we used those names and wrote letters back and forth." She laughed, thinking of her youth.

I thought about my hunch. It checked out. "Mia Lee is old granny Minakami!" I blurted out.

"Correct, Kazu," Yūsuke's grandma answered. "I believe you know Ms. Minakami, don't you? You ought to call her something besides old granny." She frowned.

Yūsuke and Akari both seemed bewildered. They had no clue who Ms. Minakami was.

"I always thought Mia Lee was a lovely name," Yūsuke's grandmother went on. "I envied her. She was a class ahead of me. She was stylish and smart, and everyone wanted to be like her."

"Wow, really?" Yūsuke couldn't quite believe that his grandmother had envied someone.

"She finished school and then moved to Tokyo. I heard that she wanted to be a manga artist, which was still quite rare for a woman back then.

"Anyway, just about the time I stopped getting news of her, her parents gave copies of a magazine to their neighbors and acquaintances. They must have been proud of their daughter. I think I read it too, but . . ."

She shook her head, not sure she remembered.

"So my grandpa got a copy of *Daisy* from Ms. Minakami's family," I said. Then he gave it to Mrs. Andō.

"Is Mia Lee, Ms. Minakami, still alive?" Akari asked, looking from Yūsuke's grandma to me.

"She lives right here in town, fit as a fiddle," I grumbled.

"Kazu. Are you mad or something?" Yūsuke asked.

I was scowling again. And with good reason. Everything that was wrong was Ms. Minakami's fault: "The Moon Is on the Left" had no ending, and Akari might vanish at any instant.

"Don't you think she could have written the rest of the story, even though she moved back here?" I asked. I wanted them to think I was interested only in the story.

"She came home because her father fell ill. They lived near where your place is now, Kazu, but their store was on Minami Ōdori," Yūsuke's grandma told us. "It was a furniture store. Ms. Minakami had to take it over, so she must have been busy.

"She closed it some time ago now. It used to be in that spot where the convenience store and community parking lot are now."

We nodded. That area was large. The Minakamis had sold furniture, so they must have had a big store.

"She was new to the family business and to managing a staff, and she bore a heavy responsibility," Yūsuke's grandma continued. "I'm sure she had no time to write."

I understood. But what about now?

We reached Yūsuke's parking lot before five. His dad must have floored it, because we got home much faster than usual.

"Kazu, are you rushing somewhere?" Yūsuke asked when he saw me running in the opposite direction from Kimyō Temple Alley.

"I'm going to Ms. Minakami's place," I answered.

As soon as I said that, Akari ran over. "You're going to see Mia Lee?" she asked.

"If you're going, so am I!" Yūsuke said.

"Me too!" Akari echoed.

Akari's eyes sparkled. Mia Lee officially had fans.

The three of us ended up barging into Minami Heights. Ms. Minakami was home, in apartment 902. So was Kiriko.

"Kazu, I hear you came yesterday as well," Ms. Minakami said through the intercom, before buzzing us into the building.

When she opened her door and saw all of us, she asked, "What's this? Have you all come to call me 'bullheaded'?"

171

It seemed the super had relayed my message.

Before Ms. Minakami could scold me, Akari pushed me aside and asked, "Are you Ms. Mia Lee?"

I hoped Akari would control herself. I had no clue what had become of the Kimyō Temple statuette, and I did not want Ms. Minakami knowing Akari's identity.

"We're fans of yours," Yūsuke said. "We love 'The Moon Is on the Left.'"

Ms. Minakami stood there, clearly in shock. "How . . . how did you know I wrote that?" she asked, looking from one of us to the other.

"It took ages to figure out," I answered. "I had to call your publisher in Tokyo." I made a show of exhaling loudly.

Resigned, Ms. Minakami let the three of us inside.

"We read 'The Moon Is on the Left' in *Daisy*," Yūsuke explained.

"It was amazing!" Akari added.

"What happens next?" I asked.

Ms. Minakami looked at the three of us, perplexed.

She had assumed that we'd come about the Kimyō Temple statuette. Now she saw that wasn't the case. Good. If I said nothing about the connection between Kimyō Temple and "The Moon Is on the Left," she might never know about Akari.

"Kazu, how did you and your friends find a story from so long ago?" Ms. Minakami asked. All three of us were red from the sun and so excited that we looked ready to burst. She served us cold juice.

"I was looking up stuff on my grandpa for summer homework," I said. "My first topic didn't work out." I knew she would know what I meant.

"That's how we came across 'The Moon Is on the Left,'" I continued. "And Yūsuke's grandma told us that Mia Lee is actually you." I turned to Yūsuke. "Oh yeah, this is my friend Yūsuke, from Takamatsuya in Minami Ōdori—"

"Oh, you're Tomi-chan's grandson, are you?" Ms. Minakami said to him. "Both Gen-chan and Tomi-chan had such nice grandchildren," she added.

"And this is Akari Shinobu, a classmate from the neighborhood—" I said, introducing Akari. I nearly mentioned where she lived, same as I'd done for Yūsuke. Then I realized this was a bad idea, because her address is Kimyō Temple Alley.

"Anyway, the three of us read your story, and we want to know what happens next."

Yūsuke and Akari nodded fervently. Their eyes shone with expectation. I felt just as eager, but I was suspicious of Ms. Minakami. I had a serious bone to pick with this granny.

"Did you write the rest of the story?"

"If you didn't write it, did you finish it in your imagination?"

Yūsuke and Akari leaned forward as they spoke.

"Well, I stopped writing a long time ago," Ms. Minakami answered.

"You *always* do this!" I said, sulking. "You never answer yes or no. Which is it?!" I demanded.

I was in a foul mood. Yūsuke and Akari looked puzzled, wondering what had come over me, but I could hardly bother with that. I was fighting mad.

"You're so—unclear!" I said.

"Come, come, there's no need to lose your grip. Until now, I had forgotten all about 'The Moon Is on the Left.'"

Ms. Minakami pursed her lips.

"If you forgot about it, then please try to remember now! Is there an ending?" I asked.

"I gave it some thought once, but—"

"Aren't you ashamed of yourself, stopping in the middle like that?"

"I'm not ashamed at all."

"That's a lie! There's no way you could write so much of a story, and then stop and not care."

By now, Yūsuke was yanking on my collar. He couldn't believe my reaction. "Settle down, Kazu," he said. "What's gotten into you?"

But I had no plans to give up without a fight. I'd done that once already with the Kimyō Temple statuette.

"You told me you live life so as not to have any regrets," I said to Ms. Minakami. "That you would never want to come back to life, because you'll die with no regrets."

"I said that, did I?" said Ms. Minakami. She looked away.

Akari sensed something. Her mouth formed an "O."

"Yes. Now write the rest of the story," I said to Ms. Minakami.

"Yes, please!" Akari pleaded. "I so want to read it!"

"Me too!" Yūsuke added.

Yūsuke and Akari both bowed.

"And write it quickly. We're in a hurry," I said. "Akari, you have the copy, right?"

I shoved the copy at Ms. Minakami.

"You probably remember it, but here's the story up to the December issue."

Ms. Minakami neither agreed nor declined, but I shot her a glare and stood to go.

When we were outside the apartment building, Yūsuke whistled at me. "Kazu, I've never seen you get that worked up before! You were in a zone."

"You and Ms. Minakami acted like grandma and grand-son," Akari said, giggling.

"I can't stand her," I said. My hands clenched into fists.

"Are you kidding? I thought you two were close, or maybe related," Yūsuke said. He was clueless as usual.

"I'm going to her place every day from now on to make sure she writes it," I said.

Akari looked concerned, or maybe happy. It was hard to tell. "Yeah, I want to read it," was all she said.

I wanted to cry. Her future reminded me too much of the story as it was.

"Kazu, you can't boss Ms. Minakami around just because you know her. You made me nervous in there," Yūsuke said. "If I said that stuff to my grandma, I'd be a goner."

"Ms. Minakami's got quite a few years left," I commented.

"Yep. My grandma too," Yūsuke replied. He nodded happily. Clearly, despite his grandmother's crossness, he loved her. But I still hated Ms. Minakami.

The next day, my summer vacation got hectic.

In the morning, I went to radio exercises and checked to make sure Akari was alive. She was. Next, I headed to Minami Heights. I rang the bell for apartment 902 and woke up Ms. Minakami.

"Kazu, I am not an early riser!" she whined through the intercom.

"This is no time to sleep," I reminded her.

"Do you plan not to let me sleep at all?" she asked.

"You've slept thousands of hours before today. That should be enough. Wake up and finish the story."

"Writing without sleep is impossible."

"There's no time."

"I can't just whip up an ending like magic."

"You could if you tried."

The two of us had a yelling match over the intercom. This routine repeated itself the next day. And the next. The super began to buzz me in as far as Ms. Minakami's hallway to avoid disturbing the people coming and going.

We began to have the same shouting match on the intercom by Ms. Minakami's door.

Finally, on the sixth day, she gave in: "OK, OK! I'll write. I promise. Stop waking me every morning! I write at night!"

Akari was still coming to radio exercises with a smile on her face, and she practiced her swimming at the school pool.

After Ms. Minakami promised that she would write the rest of the story, I began to call her apartment in the evenings.

"Kazu. You're driving me crazy," she said on the phone.

"Crazy is as crazy does. We have no time!" I said.

"Stop calling every day!"

"I can't just sit here waiting for you."

"Boys like you won't make any friends, you know that?"

"Some people love boys like me."

All we did was bicker every time we talked.

I lost count of how many days passed. The August season of Obon began, and for the first time ever, Ms. Minakami called me rather than the other way around.

"Listen, Kazu, I had plans to travel over Obon. This story has wrecked my trip."

"Did you finish it?"

"I don't know if it will meet your high standards, but, yes, I've finished."

"I'll be over with Akari and Yūsuke," I said, hanging up. I shot out of the house.

~~~~

Ms. Minakami invited us in and handed us a stack of papers. They'd been printed out, so she clearly knew how to use a computer. I handed the stack to Akari. Ms. Minakami looked tired. She gave a yawn, and Kiriko yawned too.

Akari started reading immediately. Yūsuke watched her, barely able to wait his turn.

"Shall I, um, rub your shoulders?" I asked Ms. Minakami reluctantly.

She laughed. "No need. I'm content to have your phone calls stop."

"I drove you crazy, huh?"

"Um, *yes*, you certainly did. Which reminds me, Kazu—I might need a favor from you later on. When that time comes, I hope you can help me out."

I got a bad feeling. "What do you need?" I asked.

"Nothing to be concerned with today," she answered.

Ms. Minakami lifted Kiriko to her lap. Kiriko meowed as if to agree with everything her owner had said.

Ms. Minakami's favor could hardly be nothing. As I considered that, Akari and Yūsuke finished the first page and handed it to me. I forgot all about the favor. The new manuscript even had more illustrations of Adi and the other characters.

As Yūsuke began to chat merrily with Ms. Minakami about his grandma, I began to read.

Chapter Eleven

"The Moon Is on the Left"

PART THREE

Having taken her son back to the castle, Stonebird descended the staircase. I sprang away from the door of the prince's cell.

Brushing snow from her head and body, Stonebird peered into the prince's cell window. "Where is the pearl, then?" she asked.

"You promised to free us," he replied, searching for me from the corner of his eye.

The prince was bluffing. He did not know the exact location of the pearl. But he, the woman in the next cell, and I had an idea. I had a feeling something was in the area we had discussed. I didn't know if it would lead us to the pearl, but I sensed it was our only hope. I nodded to show this—though I felt my heart pound.

The prince saw me nod. "Let us out," he commanded.

"I'll keep my promise," Stonebird replied. "But I wonder if you really want that. You'll never survive outside."

"Better than withering away in here!"

"Really? Well, I suppose a prince should have a princely way of dying." Stonebird hunched her shoulders.

She seemed to harbor a fondness for the prince, whom she had once made call her "Mother."

"Where is the pearl?" she asked again.

"You will find it below the cliffs at the north shore, toward the east," the prince told her.

"That's the area *you* searched long ago, isn't it? Can she find it?"

Stonebird looked at me. I nodded vaguely, knowing that I would be the one to dive.

"I see we're going to need both of you," Stonebird said. She took the key from her pocket and unlocked the door to the prince's cell. I heard a bang.

"There's no way I can take you both on my broom. We'll use the boat." Stonebird beckoned the prince out with her hand.

"Let me out too. Let me out!" the woman in the other cell cried. "Don't leave me here alone like this! I can't take it anymore!"

"The three of us will go together," the prince declared.

"She'll just get in the way," said Stonebird. "But suit yourself, you'll be lucky to survive another day as it is." Stonebird sniffed and opened the woman's cell.

The woman ventured out, gingerly feeling her way. I took hold of one of her hands with its black fingernails like mine.

We went upstairs and stepped onto the terrace. The surroundings were so bright I could barely open my eyes. Morning had arrived and the blizzard had passed. Stonebird had gotten covered in snow as she flew back, so the weather must just have settled. Pure white stretched as far as we could see.

A boat sat on the frozen lake. A rope ladder hung from the terrace down to the boat. Without a qualm, the prince climbed down to the boat. When I led the woman to the ladder, she too managed to ease herself down slowly. After Stonebird and I got in, there was still enough space for several more people. My mind raced, remembering my first boat ride. I wondered if I would feel the same dreadful sensation in my stomach. Worrying about that was easier than wondering what would become of us if we didn't find the pearl.

Stonebird stood at the bow of the boat. The prince stood at the stern, as though his position were obvious, and prodded the ice with a long pole. The boat slid along at a steady clip, slicing through the crisp air. The wind no longer blew. Just as I was thinking I could handle the sliding motion, the ice beneath us cracked, and we eased into the water. It was as the prince had said: the lake did not completely freeze. I gripped the side of the boat. Stonebird squatted and held onto the sides as well. I realized that she was used to riding her broom and must get seasick on boats, like me. The prince placed the pole in the boat and took up an oar. Then he rowed us through the water. The boat rocked a bit, though not as much as when I had crossed the river. His rowing was skillful, but still I shuddered.

"Your strokes are steady as ever," Stonebird commented, turning.

"I rowed every day as a child," the prince answered.

His voice had a hint of cheer in it. Perhaps he was recalling his childhood, when he believed that Stonebird was his mother, or perhaps he was happy to exercise his muscles after so many years in the dungeon. Maybe he was just happy to breathe fresh air again. As he moved the boat forward with confidence, his now-scrawny body did not seem weak.

"I wonder how many children have ridden in this boat and dived in the lake," the prince murmured.

"I was the only one in my time," the woman said, turning her sightless eyes to him.

"You were special," the prince told her. He looked meaningfully from the woman to me.

He seemed to imply that she and I shared a unique quality. I too had dived alone.

"What happened to the other children?" I asked warily. "Did they get shut in the dungeon and die?" I almost didn't want to hear the answer, but I could not stop myself from asking.

"No, none of them lived. Something in the mud of the lake bed disagreed with them—though I've never seen any dead fish rot and float on this lake," said Stonebird, shaking her head. "I could count on one hand the number of children who made it to the dungeon."

"So, all the children you bought died," I said, my body shaking as I understood.

"Yes, they did," the witch answered, nodding and bowing her head. "Except one. One child was utterly useless. I really misjudged that one! He disappointed me. He seemed so agile and observant."

Stonebird clicked her tongue in disgust. She spoke as if the child were nothing more than an apple she had bought and then found to be rotten inside.

The prince looked up at Stonebird's words. He had lived with her since the day after his birth. Surely, he remembered the child she spoke of.

What had happened to this child who had proved "useless"? I wondered. He seemed not to have perished here, but I was too scared to ask what had become of him. I surmised that she had not killed him. The prince and the woman had been shut in the dungeon, but she had at least spared their lives.

The boat reached a place where we could see the northern cliffs. The prince looked at me occasionally to check the direction. I pointed with a finger that was out of Stonebird's view. The place I wondered about was at the eastern end of the cliffs, beneath a spot where a towering gingko tree flamed yellow in autumn. When I looked at the tree, the prince nodded.

"The pearl can be found in an opening below that tree," he said. "If it's still in there, that is." He skillfully spoke as if my idea were his.

The boat stopped at a patch of thick ice. From here, it seemed possible to walk on the ice to the shore.

"You can't find it yourself, can you?" Stonebird said to the prince, seeming to suspect something. She looked at me.

I removed the threadbare dress I was wearing. The hempen one I arrived in had grown too small in recent months, so I was wearing a castoff. I was taller now.

No one asked if I was cold or expressed concern about me diving in frigid water. The woman and prince must have endured temperatures exactly like this. I was used to it too. Once I got in the water, it seemed warmer than it had in the boat.

In the area I had glimpsed through the lake's murk, something or someone waited. I had sensed a presence here beneath the surface. I didn't know if there was a

connection to the pearl, but this was the only place in the lake where I had ever sensed anything. The prince and the woman hadn't mentioned a creature living here, so perhaps it—whatever it was—had not been alive when they were diving.

Unlike the east shore, where I had always searched, the lake bed off the north shore had large boulders. The cliffs seemed to be crumbling into the water. Today I could sense nothing through the muck. I returned to the surface for air. To head toward the cliffs, I needed to swim under thick ice. I didn't know if I could hold my breath long enough. The prince and Stonebird spotted me. The prince nodded firmly.

I breathed deeply and dove again. Dodging submerged boulders, I swam toward the cliffs. Sometimes my hands or feet struck rock, but I could still half-see. As I kicked with my legs, thinking I could go further, I struck something sharp and cut myself. A rock, perhaps. Pain shot through my right calf. I kept going.

When I reached the base of the cliffs, I detected movement. A large boulder seemed to be swaying in the current even though the current was weak here. I decided to turn back when my right leg got stuck. Caught, to be more accurate. Though not between two rocks. Had something grabbed me?

No sooner did I wonder this than I felt teeth sink into me. I would have screamed, but I was underwater. I kicked with my left leg at the mouth that bit my right, when an arm swatted my leg away. I thought it might be a giant fish, but it had arms. When I leaned

toward it, thinking to pry its jaws
loose with my hands, I saw a large
red eye. The creature had jet-black
fur and no ears—a face like a rat.
It swung my body about. Its fangs
enveloped my leg. I needed air. But I
couldn't rise to the surface.

As I began to lose consciousness, I suddenly floated free. I
shot to the surface and gulped in air. I saw the
blind woman gripping the rim of the boat and staring at the water. Stonebird frowned next to her. The
prince wasn't there. Then I saw him surface in front
of me, gripping the long pole from the boat. He must
have worried when he didn't see me resurface.

"What was that monster? A giant otter?" He glanced
around wide-eyed.

"Is something living in the water?" Stonebird asked
as she peered closely at the lake.

"Are you all right?" the blind woman shouted, her
voice echoing all around.

I began to nod, to agree it must be a large otter,
when it bit my leg again and pulled me under.

"It smelled her blood!" I heard the prince say.

The beast had been lured by blood and followed
me. It seemed to have fixed on me as its prey. This
time it would not let go so easily. As it dragged me
through the water, I could do nothing but flail my legs
and arms helplessly.

Above my head loomed a large boulder; as if to circle the base of it, the beast rose to the surface with

me in its mouth. In the base of the boulder yawned a cave. *That cave must be the animal's nest,* I thought. There was a shelf of rock inside, on which the beast flung me. Above the shelf there seemed to be an air hole. I could breathe now and see in the light.

I can breathe, but I could die here, I thought. I ground my teeth, angry. I had once thought that eating well was reason enough to live. I had changed. I felt different now.

Once I was on the shelf, the creature released my leg. It seemed to want hold of a softer spot. With a low growl, it lunged for my throat. I threw a rock at its head. I heard a pop, but the beast stopped only an instant before coming at me again. Furiously, I felt for more stones as I scrunched backward on my bottom. All the rocks were too small. Then my hand came upon something sharp. The beast attacked again. Before I knew it, I was stabbing its red eye with what seemed like a needle. The beast persisted. It wanted my throat. I thought I was done for. Suddenly, the animal's body was dragged away from me. It dropped from the rock into the water.

I could see the prince pulling the beast's leg. It began to attack him. With the needle in my hand, I jumped into the water. But before I could stab the crea-ture again, the prince slashed its belly with a dagger. The cave filled with the smell of blood. The beast's body sank to the bottom.

"You saved my life," I said as we returned to the rock shelf.

"Let's rest here a minute," the prince replied. He pushed me onto the ledge and clambered up. "We have to stop the bleeding." He used the dagger to cut a strip from his shirt, and he wrapped my leg.

"Where did you get that?" I asked, glancing at the blade.

"Stonebird loaned it to me," he replied. "Where did you get that pin?"

My hand still gripped it, unable to open. As I eased my fingers off one by one, I answered, "It was here. I felt it with my hand."

The needle flashed gold and had a blue stone at one end. I realized it was thicker than a sewing needle.

"We used to find those often in the lake, when I was small," the prince told me. "It's a weapon disguised as a woman's hairpin."

The prince now turned to explore the rock shelf. I got up and did the same.

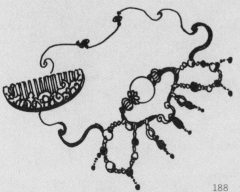

We searched the shelf on all fours.

"It's here!" The prince held up a pearl attached to a chain. It was the moon that Stonebird sought.

"It's gigantic!" I said. It was so beautiful it took my breath away. Along with the pearl and pin, we also found a jeweled hair comb carved from an animal's horn. The creature had hoarded these objects.

"At last . . ." I went limp with relief.

"You were right," the prince replied, clapping my shoulder.

"Should we really give the pearl to Stonebird?" I asked.

"Well, we agreed that if we were released—"

"But her spell will be complete! Instead of you, Stonebird's son will become king!"

"I could care less about becoming king."

Gripping the pearl, the prince dove back into the water.

I had no time to tell him that if Stonebird's son should become king, the world would grow dark. As I made to follow him, I remembered the hairpin I still clutched in my hand. It would be enough to give Stonebird the pearl, I decided. I stuck my arm up through the cave's air hole. I felt ice-cold air above, and snow. I stabbed the pin and comb in the snow near the hole.

"You found it," Stonebird said, her eyes flashing, as we hauled ourselves into the boat.

The prince held out the pearl, as large as my palm. The witch snatched it hungrily.

"Mine at last!" She giggled. Then she cackled, unable to staunch the emotions that welled deep inside her.

The blind woman found me with her hands and wordlessly touched my head, shoulders, arms, and legs, checking me. It was the first time I had been examined that way. I didn't mind it.

"You made us a promise. Now release us." The prince looked toward the shore.

"Push the boat over there. You can cross to the rocks." Stonebird pointed to the west shore of the lake. From there, we could walk the frozen surface to the cliffs beyond.

The boat slid onto the ice again. The three of us disembarked. Stonebird took the pole from the prince and turned the boat around. She did not look back.

The three of us watched for a while. We watched as birds cried noisily and circled like smoke above Stonebird's mansion. The prince looked not only at the mansion, but also at Stonebird's back as it grew smaller and smaller. It must have been hard for him; after all, he had once believed her to be his mother.

Though I had dived, today I would not be able to warm my body by a stove, and I soon began to shiver. My bare feet grew numb on the frozen ground. The blind woman wrapped her arms around me. The prince was wet too. At this rate, we would freeze to death before we starved.

"We're free," the prince muttered, seeming to come back to himself. "No shoes, but we're free!"

Forcing his eyes from the place where he had lived for twenty years, beginning with his second day of life, the prince looked at us.

"And we have no place to go," I reminded him. But his high spirits were catching. I knew now that living meant more than surviving. With no shoes and no shelter, I stood in possession of my own will and strength. I was as happy as the prince himself.

"We need to warm up. Say, I believe there's a house south of the lake," said the prince. "Let's try to find help."

The prince turned resolutely from the shore.

"I remember that place," the blind woman said, nodding. "I only ever saw an old man there, though. I wonder if he lives alone."

I had never dived on the south side, so I didn't know of any house. That was how big the lake was, and that house was the closest shelter.

The sun sank rapidly. Snow began falling again. Still, we walked on toward the south. My body grew numb through and through, and my legs barely functioned. The blind woman held one arm tight around my shoulders, and the prince held her by her other hand. The two of us moved as if pulled along by him. It was easier to walk the frozen fields than the lake surface.

At times we got stuck in deep snow and struggled to free ourselves. I badly wanted to go to sleep in those snowdrifts.

"Adi! Wake up! Wake up!" the woman roused me each time, slapping my cheeks. Somehow, I would open my eyes and move my legs again. My mind went blank. Except for one thought: How did she know my name? I had never told her.

⁓

I was naked. The woman was naked too, her body wrapped around mine to warm me inside a worn wool blanket. I had slept.

When I stirred, she spoke. "Good! You've come to." Deeply relieved, she rubbed my back with one hand.

This room was not as warm as Stonebird's mansion, but a fire crackled in a crumbling stove, and a roof sheltered us. We had reached the house on the south side—though it was more hut than house. Snow blew in through cracks in the walls and formed mounds inside. Still, this was the kind of house I was used to.

"These are men's clothes and have holes in them, but there's still some wear left," the woman said. She gave me a shirt and trousers that were faded, but dry.

"You might have frostbite. Put your feet in here." The prince poured lukewarm water into a basin for me.

"The man who lived here must have left several years ago," he said. "Everything's coated in dust." He brought some dried-out potatoes from the pantry. "We started a fire. We have a place to sleep. There's even food to eat," he added. "Not bad!"

The prince put the potatoes in the pot and hung it over the fire.

The potatoes were rock-hard, even after we boiled them, but having something to put in our mouths gave us peace.

"If we sell that pin the giant otter had, we'll have food till spring," the prince said. He planned to retrieve the pin from the cliffs north of the lake when the snow stopped.

"Adi? You found something besides the pearl?" the woman asked, turning her blind eyes toward me.

I said yes, and then asked, "Why do you know my name?"

"I'm Hami. You don't remember me, do you? I knew you were kin from the moment Stonebird said you were Polonia. Polonia is what they call us in this land," the blind woman answered.

Hami was the name of my eldest sibling.

"You're my sister? My sister!" I gripped her hand, with its fingernails like mine.

"That's right, Adi," she answered. She embraced me. Her embrace was warm. *My sister.* I had found her in the last place on earth I could have imagined. The hands that had checked me when I came out of the lake had been the hands of my own flesh and blood.

"They say Polonia have ancestors who died, then came back to life," the prince explained. "Your bodies are different from other people's. The sludge in the lake doesn't affect you as it did those other children."

I realized that the people the prince called Polonia were those of us who had minded the royal graves.

"My eyes were sharper than the other children's, but they worsened more quickly," Hami said. "But, Adi, your sight should be unaffected. You dove for less than a year."

Hami brushed tears from my cheek with her finger.

"So we really are descendants of the reborn," I muttered.

"I hear that Polonia have an especially strong attachment to life," the prince said. "Must be because your ancestors tasted death once. They wished to live, no matter what. But they say that if your desire for life goes out, you fade away instantly. I'm amazed at how Hami here has clung to life, despite everything she's faced."

The prince turned to my sister. I wanted to tell her just how his eyes looked at that moment, but I did not have the words.

My sister Hami had been taken to the capital and sold when she was ten. The buyer had been a prominent purveyor of furs.

"I was happier not being home, just as Father had said," Hami told me. "I had plenty to eat. At first, I only did household chores. The furrier and his wife took a liking to me, and they began to teach me how to handle furs in the shop. At that time, Stonebird came to buy a pelt and saw my fingernails. She asked to buy me, but the furrier said no. He knew she was a witch.

"Stonebird stole me."

Hami had dived in the lake for four years, then been shut in the dungeon for three. She was now nineteen.

"But because I was in Stonebird's dungeon, I found you," Hami said to me. "There's no way I will die now. I'm going to survive!" She embraced me again.

It was as the prince had said: Hami had been sold by our father, stolen by Stonebird, gone blind, and been imprisoned in the dungeon—yet she wished to live. Seeing her, I knew that I could do the same. I had found her. I had a roof over my head. Potatoes to eat. The potatoes meant a potato patch waited under the snow.

"That's the spirit!" the prince said. "We can't die in a place like this! I've got to make a trip to the north shore. Long ago, I made a promise to someone there." He nodded determinedly.

It was the first day of the New Year, and it was a day filled with hope.

The weather cleared only on the morning of New Year's Day. From then on, every day the sky was overcast, and snow floated down.

The prince and I made trips to the cliffs on the north shore of the lake.

The first day we stood atop the cliffs, we saw Stonebird fly away on her broom, holding a tube-shaped object. The tube had to be the rolled-up spell-tapestry, now complete. Where had she taken it? We never spotted her again.

The next day, the birds that had circled Stonebird's mansion so noisily disappeared. Not one remained. They seemed to have understood that Stonebird would never return. Now that her spell was complete, she had no use for the lake.

I climbed down from the northern cliffs and searched for the pin I had hidden near the air hole.

"Be careful. There's nothing but thick ice below. If you slip and fall, you could hurt yourself badly."

The prince tied a rope around me made of old rags.

On the third day, I found the pin. I also found the carved comb.

Since my sister had lived for a time in the capital, she knew the geography of our area well.

"This lake sits east of the capital. To get there requires half a day—no, a whole day, in this snow. In the capital you can sell these items for a high price, but you have barely eaten, and the journey will be hard. Before the capital there's a large village. How about selling the things there?"

The prince and I trudged through the snow to that village. My sister had been right; it was tough going. When we finally reached the village, it had taken us half a day, and we could barely move our legs from exhaustion.

To me, the village might well have been the capital. It bustled with activity. It probably served as a fortification in times of battle; its residents and passing travelers seemed rough. A group of bandits called "Wolves' Teeth" sometimes attacked here, we learned. A rich resident had been robbed just recently. The prince and I checked the large, central square of the village but doubted we could sell baubles there; the gazes of the men were so threatening that we thought we might get robbed ourselves.

We quietly showed our goods to women who looked well off. After several had passed us by, a woman who had a servant with her stopped. She showed interest in both the pin and the comb.

"Perhaps this one." She reached for the pin. The prince told her that it had been a weapon years ago, but she seemed to want it for her hair. Suddenly, I did not wish to part with it. I had fought off the loathsome otter beast with this pin. It symbolized how I had fought for my life.

"The comb looks much nicer on you," I told the woman. I slid the comb, made of black animal horn and sparkling jewels, into the woman's red hair. The prince seemed to sense my attachment to the pin and nodded, agreeing. The woman bought the comb.

"We can live on this much money for a while," the prince said. The amount we had received was less than my sister thought the comb would fetch, but we had done well for amateurs.

We drank hot soup at a street stall, and then bought all the provisions we could carry and headed back to the hut. When we arrived, late at night, my sister greeted us with a look of relief.

We couldn't really eat to our hearts' content, but we now had enough food not to starve. The next supply we needed was firewood. The prince and I returned to the forest we had passed through on our way to the village and gathered branches we thought would burn. This became our routine.

On clearer days, the prince would also build a fire atop the north cliffs. He did not say why, but when he lit the fire, he would get a happy, faraway look in his eyes. I could not understand why he would waste our firewood this way, but my sister said to let him do as he liked.

Stonebird did not reappear. The witch had definitely abandoned her lakeside mansion.

Chapter Twelve

"The Moon Is on the Left"

PART FOUR

Several days passed after that. On nicer days the prince kept lighting his fires. We soon found that we could not collect enough firewood. I resolved to ask him to stop making the fires.

Then one day while he was out, we heard sounds approach.

"Is that a horse?" My sister tilted her head and listened.

I flew to a crack between the boards that we had used to seal the windows of the hut. As Hami had known, a horse was coming. Several horses, in fact. The men who rode them carried swords at their waists.

I grabbed my pin with one hand and stuck it in the string I used for a belt. In my other hand, I gripped our largest piece of firewood. I stood with Hami behind me.

"Hami, Adi."

We heard a man speak. I thought the prince had been caught by bandits, and I stiffened. Behind me, my sister put her hand to my shoulder.

"It's all right, Adi. It's the prince and he doesn't sound upset."

When we opened the door, the prince stood next to a tall man clad in heavy furs, who had a large sword.

"I have someone for you to meet," the prince told us. "This is my one ally in the world. His name is Wolf Tooth."

"The bandit!?" I asked, alarmed. I gripped the firewood again.

"Adi, don't be frightened. This man is the one who was 'useless' to Stonebird years ago. He's the child who got thrown out of the mansion!" The prince laughed merrily. I had never heard his voice so light.

"Aye, I was 'useless,' it's true," Wolf Tooth replied. "But I lived in that mansion. I'm one of you. You did well to survive that place. And you, my friend, did well to remember our promise!" Wolf Tooth used his large arm to clap the prince on the shoulder.

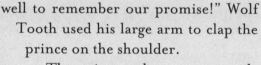

The prince, who came up only to Wolf Tooth's ear, nearly lost his balance. "You're the one who did well, recalling plans we made as children!" he answered. Tears pooled in his eyes.

"Let's tell our story someplace warmer," Wolf Tooth suggested.

"You're a wretched sight! But you made it out after all. That's something."

Wolf Tooth waved to beckon us out.

Taking only my pin, I left the hut with my sister.

Wolf Tooth's headquarters were in the capital, inside an outer wall. The area was more prosperous than any we had seen so far, yet it still had many poor people. When you opened an old wooden door in one wall, a courtyard appeared surrounded by buildings with several balconies. The buildings formed a U shape. Some wall-dwellings seemed to have five stories, others seven. Wolf Tooth's underlings lived here by the dozens, including some with families. The shouts of children echoed in the courtyard.

"My official business here is meat vending," Wolf Tooth explained. "My men and I buy game from mountain hunters and sell it at markets, or we supply it to butchers. As we travel to buy our meat, we also relieve certain people of their riches."

Wolf Tooth told us that since he ran a legitimate business, he had never been suspected of the robberies. As we sat in his warm rooms, with a huge fireplace and furniture as impressive as Stonebird's, Wolf Tooth laughed merrily. On the surface, he seemed to live much like a well-to-do merchant.

Having bathed, changed into warm clothes, and eaten till my stomach nearly burst, I listened to him and the prince in a reverie. I fingered my new dress constantly; I had never encountered such soft fabric. I couldn't believe I was wearing such a garment,

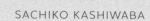

the color of sunset. Moments before, I hadn't even recognized myself in the mirror. I'd frozen when I was given fur slippers to wear with the dress. Could I really put them on?

The woman who brought me the dress said, "Next time I'll cut your hair." I must have looked as bedraggled as a stray kitten.

"Stonebird purchased me as a child and trained me to dive like you, but I swam like a rock," Wolf Tooth continued. "I really was useless. Not half a year passed before she threw me out."

He sheepishly added that he still couldn't swim.

"When I learned I would be cast out of the mansion, I made the prince promise me that if he got out too, he would send a smoke signal from the top of that cliff. And I promised I would go meet him." Wolf Tooth laughed. "Of course, I had no idea if I would even survive!"

"I'm amazed you remembered those vows between boys," the prince said to Wolf Tooth. The prince's eyes were red. He had been crying since the two were reunited.

"If you hadn't fished me out of the lake when I worked for Stonebird, I would have drowned!" Wolf Tooth replied. "A man never forgets the one who saved his life.

"But to tell the truth, those days had started to slip from my mind. I go to the village west of the lake to pick up news sometimes, as soldiers from other countries gather there. I never go to the lake itself, but I have a habit of glancing at it. When I saw the smoke rise to the sky today, my memories came rushing back. I doubted my own good sense, but I went to the cliff to investigate, and I'm glad I did!"

Wolf Tooth did not have to explain why he had become a bandit. He had been a child with no home, who was sold. One could easily imagine what had happened. I envied him the cleverness that had changed his hard life.

The prince spoke to him of Stonebird's spell.

"Has she been casting it all these years, then?" Wolf Tooth asked, surprised.

Wolf Tooth came by his name honestly; when he spoke, he showed a set of brilliant teeth.

Everyone in the room wanted nothing more now than to break Stonebird's spell.

"Is she still in her mansion, then?" Wolf Tooth asked.

I shook my head. "She's gone. She abandoned it. Even the birds have left."

"Where's that witch hiding then?" Wolf Tooth groaned. "It'll be a job to find her, it will. We might have a chance at the coronation—there'll be information about it beforehand. But it's nearly impossible to slip into the castle."

Wolf Tooth told us about the castle's corps of magicians. They used their powers to keep the entire castle hidden. No one knew where it was, even longtime residents of the capital. When Stonebird had said the prince could not reach the castle alone, she had known this. Even she wasn't able to come and go at will; on the last day of each year, the magic that hid the castle weakened, and that's how she'd been able to meet her son's ghost.

Wolf Tooth told us that he would seek out some gossip. Nothing is as unreliable as gossip, of course, but there's often truth hiding in it. Yet an antidote to Stonebird's spell would be hard to come by. We were as stuck as we had been before.

Our dilemma burdened us, but the days still passed. The window of the room my sister and I shared looked out over city streets. Before, I had wakened to the cries of raucous birds, but now human voices and horse carts roused me. I helped with cleaning and cooking in Wolf Tooth's house, yet I still had time on my hands. My sister thought often of the furrier who had trained her, and, though we never exactly set out to find him, she and the prince and I took many walks around the capital. We sometimes joined Wolf Tooth's partners in practicing combat and archery techniques in the courtyard. The prince drilled with a sword, and I used my special pin.

One day, I watched a boy practice in the courtyard using blow darts. About five years of age, he had just learned to hit his farthest target.

"That's the way!" said Wolf Tooth, who watched him with me. "Even some adults can't do that."

The boy's face flushed, and he ran from the court-yard, seeming embarrassed. But he returned shortly, tugging his mother's hand. The boy demonstrated his skills again, and his young mother embraced him, her whole face beaming.

It seemed so natural that a child would want his mother to see what he could do. And for a mother to admire her child.

"I bet you anything Stonebird will come see her son at the coronation," I blurted out. "She'll want to see his ghost come back to life."

I thought of the way I had heard Stonebird speak to her son. Her voice had grown thick with affection.

"You think she'll come to the ceremony, then?" Wolf Tooth responded. "Even a witch can't get in eas-ily, especially at a coronation. No one enters without an invitation."

"I'll bet she can get one," I told him. "The coro-nation itself is happening because of her spell. She might have stitched herself into the tapestry."

"You're right," Wolf Tooth said, nodding. "She spent twenty years on that spell. She must have made herself part of it, in a role that would guarantee an invitation."

"I'm sure she has a cover, like you," the prince told Wolf Tooth. "A public role that rouses no suspicion, which would get her invited."

"And she could have a base besides the lake," Wolf Tooth added, nodding now with certainty.

We'd wondered that too. But there was still no way for us to find her.

A royal proclamation soon announced the coronation.

Rumors spread like wildfire.

"A tapestry appeared in the castle storehouse. They say it shows a coronation!"

"The king and queen in the tapestry look exactly like the real king and queen!"

"They say the prince who disappeared at birth will return at the ceremony!"

"He'll appear when the moon shines through the window above the throne, on the left!"

"He has spent all of these years in the land of the fairies. A fortune-teller predicted he would not grow up well in this country."

"No, they say he's dwelt in the land of ice on the far side of the sea!"

"He must be so clever, kind, and handsome!"

"The king and queen can't wait to see him!"

"The tapestry will be displayed all over the capital!"

Rumors of the tapestry display were true. Several days before the coronation, we learned the tapestry would be carried to each of the capital's main squares for public viewing. The residents of the capital, who never got to see inside the castle itself, awaited the display eagerly.

With little progress in our planning, the day of the tapestry display arrived.

The prince, my sister and I walked to a nearby square to wait. It seemed everyone in the city had turned out. "I won't be able to see it anyway!" my sister moaned, but she still came with us. We stood together, as crowds nearly squashed us straining for a glimpse.

The tapestry had been mounted on a wooden frame, which now appeared in the square held by two soldiers. Twenty guards stood around it, with spears at the ready. The townspeople gathered around the spearmen. It seemed nearly impossible to get a close look at the tapestry, but my sharp eyes served me well even here.

The moon shone through the window to the left of the throne. The embroidered people in the scene, no matter how small, were meticulously detailed: some

even had moles. *Stonebird must be among them,* I thought, but as I searched for her, the soldiers holding the frame, along with the guards, left the square.

The onlookers scrambled to follow them, as a voice called out.

"Hami! Hami, is that you?"

A white-haired, red-faced, portly man gazed at my sister and her unseeing eyes.

"Sir!" My sister raised her hand toward him.

"Hami, you're alive! But your eyes—" The man took my sister's hand. Before she could say a word, he continued. "The furrier and his wife worried terribly. You've come at a bad time for them, but your being here will lift their spirits. Come, let's go to them at once!"

The man began to walk. As we kept pace with him, my sister introduced him as the furrier's supervisor of workers.

"You say it's a bad time," she said. "Has something happened at the shop?"

"The master is overwhelmed," he replied. "The reason has to do with that tapestry!" He glared toward the cloth as the procession left the square. Then, showing us to the shop, he explained.

The furrier my sister worked for had recently gained permission to enter the castle. He had agreed to make the mantle, or cloak, for the queen to wear to the coronation. Using the best fur in his shop, he had created and delivered a fine mantle as requested. The queen was pleased at first, but the day before the tapestry display, he had been ordered to remake the mantle from scratch.

Belief in the tapestry had swelled as people realized that even moles on the invited guests were embroidered exactly. The king now desired that everyone attending the coronation look exactly as in the tapestry. The queen's mantle in the tapestry appeared black with a shiny finish. The furrier had been told to make an exact replica. The supervisor had come to view the tapestry today to confirm the shade of black.

The queen shown in the tapestry appeared larger than the other participants, and she definitely wore a black mantle. It had pearl-like objects on it that sparkled like stars at night. I had seen this myself.

"The first mantle we delivered was premium sable, in a rich brown-black," the supervisor explained. "A darker mantle than that will be impossible to create. The scattering of pearls we can handle. But even if we order furs from other shops, none will be large enough. The master is beside himself."

If the master did not succeed, he added, his shop and his very life would be threatened.

"Can you not seam the furs?" the prince asked.

"Not for royalty," my sister explained. "Every mantle for the castle is worked from one large fur."

"Can there be an animal with a hide that large? It would have to be a monster!"

The prince and I looked at each other.

"If we can help make a mantle, can we get into the castle?" the prince asked.

"Of course! Do you have an idea about the hide?"
the supervisor asked.

"Yes!" The prince and I answered at once.

Wolf Tooth's underlings gathered by the dozens and
launched ten boats onto the lake. The prince and I dove
again. We had killed the otter beast some thirty days
before. Stonebird had told us that dead fish in the lake
never decayed, but we wondered if fish had nibbled at
the hide. I was glad I had not poked it all over with my
pin. We tied ropes around its legs, and the carcass was
hauled to the surface. Its wounded belly had indeed
been eaten away, but its back was intact.

"A newtoria!" exclaimed the supervisor, who had
boarded our boat with us. He wept with relief. He told
us they could make a fine mantle from this animal,
whose name we had never heard. Apparently, some
people preferred newtoria fur to all others.

The mantle made from the water beast's hide was
supple, shiny, and smooth as silk.

The mantle was completed on the afternoon of the
coronation day. The furrier agreed to take the prince,
Wolf Tooth, and me to the castle as the delivery crew.

My sister opposed the plan and grew so worried
for the prince and me that her face turned pale. She

protested that any slip-ups would put the furrier at risk. But the furrier reassured her, laughing: "Without this fur, my life would be at risk anyway!"

The prince added, "If we don't break this spell, there's no point in me being alive." He smiled.

"But I—I—"

Hami fell silent. I knew she wished to say that without the prince, she herself could not live. She loved him. He clasped her hand. I knew now that it was because of him that she had survived those years in the dungeon.

The box holding the mantle hung from a large pole. Wolf Tooth and the prince walked at the front and rear ends of the pole, bearing the weight on their shoulders. I walked ahead of them, my pin tucked in my belt. The furrier led us.

We walked a winding road to the castle. Mist appeared and obscured the road. The furrier held an oil lamp aloft. When he did so, a narrow path revealed itself, due to the magic of the castle magicians.

A gate materialized in the mist, and five castle guards looked us over.

"Aren't you a rather large group?" one questioned.

"We come bearing Her Royal Highness's mantle. It must be handled carefully. If we fail to deliver it before the ceremony, I will lose my head," the furrier replied.

The guards bid us pass.

Once we had entered the gate, others barely questioned us.

"Her Highness's mantle," we would say, and before we knew it, we had reached the interior.

We were shown to a small room in the castle and waited while an attendant took the mantle to the queen.

"Her Majesty is pleased!" the attendant reported to us. "Have a drink in the galley before you go, to celebrate."

She handed us a heavy pouch of gold coins.

The area called the galley was in fact an outdoor space with three wells, where tables were set out. Workers drew water ceaselessly from the wells, which they poured into tubs and hauled away. In a cleaning area next to the wells, servants washed vegetables, skinned animals, gutted fish, and scoured pots and pans at breakneck pace. Heat and aromas drifted from an oven beyond the wells, so that even on this winter night, everyone worked up a sweat.

The people gathered at the tables included merchants from outside, like the furrier, as well as palace servants. A man drinking wine next to me had come to deliver fish. The woman across from us was a scullery maid only now eating her lunch. Many people entered and mixed together.

Wolf Tooth intently watched two soldiers who had come to eat. He followed them as they left to resume their posts and used his powerful arms to drag them into some shadows. He and the prince soon donned their uniforms and disguised themselves as soldiers.

"We'll find the tapestry and burn it."

They disappeared into the castle.

I wanted, somehow, to slip into the coronation room.

Some carts laden with platters of food and covered in cloth stood ready to be taken away. I hid beneath one. The carts were soon wheeled to a room next door to the hall where the coronation would take place. I stole from beneath the cart to the underside of a food table and then, when the time was right, I slipped into the hall and hid beneath a platform of flowers.

Lifting the cloth draped over the platform very slightly, I looked out. As in the tapestry, I saw a window on each side of the throne. Behind the throne, Stonebird's tapestry hung on the wall. Lamps had been prepared throughout the room, but most remained unlit and the room was dim. The moon had not yet risen.

Guests began to enter. Stonebird would certainly come. I dropped the cloth and huddled beneath the platform.

I soon heard her voice.

Peeking out, I saw Stonebird flanked by women, who wore dresses with puffed sleeves and trailing hems. She had come wearing a similar dress of deep magenta and had piled her hair high on her head. She looked nothing like a witch.

"Why, Bajizu, it seems ages!" the other women said to her. "Are you quite well?"

Stonebird answered, "Yes, very well. It's a festive day!" She smiled. She must have wanted to laugh heartily. Her son would return to life and become king!

A short way off, I heard another woman whisper. "Bajizu—who's that? I've never met her."

"She's the wife of one of the ministers' distant relatives. When her husband died, she came to the capital in the minister's care. That was twenty years ago! Had you not heard?"

"She's quite frail, apparently. She often takes to her bed, and she rarely socializes."

The women's gossip turned to other people. Indeed, Stonebird seemed to have an estate in the capital and an identity to match.

The din of voices increased, and the room grew warm as the guests assembled. Beneath the flower platform, I broke a sweat.

"The king enters!"

I heard a swell of voices followed by sudden silence. I felt sure that everyone could hear my heart thudding.

The guests looked to the windows behind the throne, practically ceasing to breathe. Next to the king I saw the queen, wearing her just-completed newtoria mantle. The king and queen had both turned to watch the windows as well. Then a sliver of moon appeared in the window on the left.

The moon rose. Its glow lit the floor before the king's throne. It grew surprisingly bright.

"Ooh!" I heard muffled voices.

In the light of the moon, the kneeling figure of Stonebird's son appeared, with his head bowed. He looked exactly as in the tapestry.

"How beautiful he looks!" someone exclaimed rapturously.

The king stood to place the crown on his head.

At this rate, Stonebird's son would rule the land!

I longed to leap out and scream, "He's a fake! He's a ghost!"

But someone else—Wolf Tooth—shouted, "That prince is an impostor!"

I sprang from beneath the flower platform. I saw that Wolf Tooth had rushed into the hall alone. I wondered where the prince was.

"Trespasser!"

"Seize him!"

Guards rushed toward Wolf Tooth. He knocked out one and then another, but still more guards threatened to capture him.

I searched for the prince. I saw a torch move behind the heads of the guests. It advanced toward the throne—straight toward Stonebird's tapestry. Wolf Tooth was providing the distraction. I ran toward the torch and the prince.

Despite the presence of Wolf Tooth, the guards near the king continued to defend the throne area. One soon spotted the prince.

"Who goes there?!" The guards surrounded him.

"That prince is an impostor!" the real prince shouted. "He is the son of the witch called Stonebird—a ghost of the execution grounds!"

Guards captured the real prince. I ran to the throne from the other side. I held no flame so could not set the tapestry afire, but perhaps I could pull it from the wall and remove the pearl. Without the moon-pearl, the spell should change.

Just as everyone had ignored Wolf Tooth's accusations, so they paid no heed to the prince's. It seemed no one suspected me of possible wrongdoing, though. Only Stonebird's son, down on one knee and looking back toward the prince, suddenly turned his face my way. And then he saw me.

"You!" He stood, his face twisted in rage. He reached for me, his hand pushing past the king who stood near him.

"This prince is fake! He's the son of the witch!" I cried out. I stretched toward the tapestry, but I couldn't reach it. I felt Stonebird's son's hand on my neck.

The light from the moon in the left window did not illuminate the wall, which was directly behind the throne. Stonebird's son had come for me right in the dark patch.

"Never step out of the light!" Stonebird's voice called.

"The prince melted in the dark!" the king shouted at the same time. I heard the queen scream.

I could still see Stonebird's son in the shadows. I was not like the king and the others, who had widened their eyes in shock. As Stonebird's son tried to strangle me, I fought to breathe and managed to stab his hand with my pin.

"Ow!" He released me, his hand spurting blood. He returned to the patch of moonlight.

Everyone froze. The guests all stared at Stonebird's son. To them, he seemed to have materialized again out of the darkness.

"That prince is a pretender! A ghost of the prison!" Wolf Tooth declared.

"He's a ghost!" All the guests raised their voices.

People began running to escape Stonebird's son. The circle of guests around him widened as attendees fled.

⌒

The real prince approached the tapestry with his torch.

"The man you would crown is the son of the witch Stonebird—a ghost of the execution ground. He would return to life through the witch's spell!"

The prince thrust the torch at the tapestry.

"Mother!" Stonebird's son cried.

"I should never have let those three go," Stonebird shrieked, dropping her elegant front. Her hair spilled down and her face changed. Her dress turned back to black.

She sprinted through the hall toward the tapestry.

"She's a witch!" people screamed.

Stonebird tried to seize the prince. The soldiers who had restrained Wolf Tooth had been watching everything in a daze. Wolf Tooth knocked them all down.

The tapestry burned. As it blazed, the moon-pearl dropped to the floor of the hall. At the sound of it dropping, all the guests looked to the left window. The moon had vanished. The spell was broken.

Stonebird now battled against everyone in the castle. When a net dropped on her, she sliced through it. When a volley of arrows flew at her, she deflected it. She slid beneath slashing swords. The castle magicians arrived, hurling lightning bolts, shooting flames, and causing rockfalls. Stonebird dispelled their attacks with ease. She did not have her broom, so she couldn't flee into the sky.

The magicians lit every torch throughout the palace, determined to drive her son into the light.

I alone could see him no matter where he was. "He's there! Over there!"

People illuminated the places I pointed out so that they could see him too.

"Polonia child, let me be! What's so wrong with wanting to live again? Everyone wants to come back to life, including your ancestors! You and I are alike!

"I don't want to be a ghost anymore. I can't bear this existence. I won't do any harm. I promise! Let me go!" Stonebird's son wailed in agony.

"Spare him!" Stonebird screamed. "He's made it this far. Now that the spell is broken, he'll eventually melt back into the darkness. Spare him!"

She screeched wretchedly in despair as she saw her twenty-year spell to revive her son go up in flames.

I knew that sparing her son would cause no real harm. Since he wouldn't be crowned king, he could do little damage. He could make a new start. Then again, the prince, Hami, and Wolf Tooth had suffered terribly because of him and his mother. Children had died! How could I ever forgive that? And I did not care to think of myself or my family as like him. Then again, my Polonia ancestor had returned to life like *him*. I felt lost.

Nonetheless, I kept chasing, joining Wolf Tooth and the prince. I pursued Stonebird and I pointed out her son.

"All of you, beware! I'll never forgive you!"

Stonebird's hair sparked with her anger. Her bloodshot eyes stared right into mine.

Suddenly uncertain, I felt her words pierce my heart. *I'll never forgive you!* I froze. Stonebird would have her revenge! My knees locked. As I stood immobile, my whole body trembled.

"Fear not!" the prince shouted. "You will survive, Adi! You are Hami's sister!"

He had seen me shaking. He bid me not to give up, not to flee. He bid me to fight. He grabbed my hand and pulled me after him to chase Stonebird.

If we let her escape now, she would surely haunt us for the rest of our lives. I gritted my teeth. No. I would never live like that. I pursued her.

Stonebird and her son fled toward the castle gate. The castle magicians worked to move the gate, little by little, to trap them. When they rounded a corner in the corridor that once led to the gate, they found themselves in a courtyard. When they tried to slip out the other side, they found themselves in the galley.

The magicians seemed to have no option but to keep changing the path. But, every time they tried something, Stonebird eventually oriented herself.

"Does she not have a weakness?" Wolf Tooth shouted, clacking the teeth foretold by his name.

Then I realized something. Her name. Perhaps her weakness was water! I thought she had been seasick when she crouched with me inside her boat—but perhaps she feared the water. Maybe she couldn't swim. Maybe she, like Wolf Tooth, would sink like a brick. A *stone*.

The magicians altered her path again. When she and her son ran from the galley to the corridor, they wound up in the galley washing area.

"The wells! Chase her to a well!" I shouted.

The prince understood immediately. He clasped Stonebird to him and jumped into one of the wells with her. Though the prince soon rose to the surface, Stonebird sank. We never saw her again.

In the commotion, I spotted Stonebird's son hiding in darkness near the next well. He was sobbing and trembling. Poor man. Someone like him might have been an ancestor of mine. I could not bring myself to raise the alarm, and I let Stonebird's son get away.

Many days passed.

I had left the castle with Wolf Tooth. The prince and my sister Hami remained there. My sister wanted me to stay with her, but I found castle life stifling. So again, I was on the outside, with the castle hidden from me by magic. I could only learn of its goings-on through gossip. I heard that a coronation ceremony would be held for the formerly missing prince. And at the same time, I learned there would be a wedding. The bride-to-be was blind.

Back at Wolf Tooth's headquarters, I stared at the pearl from Stonebird's tapestry. The king had given it to me as a reward.

I didn't know what to do now. It scared me to be able to do whatever I desired. I had never been free.

I sighed. I heard another sigh from a dark spot behind me.

Stonebird's son had come into the light, but like me he did not know what to do with himself. He lurked in the capital's shadows now. He hid in darkness. The darkness near me.

He drove me crazy.

"What does it mean to embrace life?" he asked behind me. He may have been thinking of parting words from his mother. I couldn't tell if he regretted his past and desired to change, or if he had always been serious—or if he just couldn't manage without Stonebird. Whatever the reason, he kept to the shadows.

"Don't ask me!" I told him. I had no answer for him.

Wolf Tooth merely chuckled as he looked on.

CHAPTER THIRTEEN

Summer's End

"The Moon Is on the Left" ended there.

Akari clasped her hands to her chest in her signature pose, thinking.

I handed the last page to Yūsuke and began to speak, but he raised a hand to shush me. He finished reading.

We looked at each other.

"That was good," we said.

"I'm glad you're all satisfied," Ms. Minakami replied. She looked right at Akari.

Had she figured out that Akari was a ghost? I panicked, though I tried not to show it.

Akari nodded to Ms. Minakami. "Thank you for sparing Stonebird's son," she said.

Akari's hopes and dreams were all compressed in that one sentence. She had seen herself in Stonebird's son.

Ms. Minakami said nothing.

"Well, *I* didn't think the son should be spared," Yūsuke said, pouting though he had enjoyed the story.

He still knew nothing about Akari. But he might be right about the story—the ending felt a little cushy.

"Did you change the story from the one you imagined years ago?" I asked Ms. Minakami.

A woman who would burn the Kimyō Temple statuette would never have let Stonebird's son go free. Had she changed?

She answered neither Yūsuke nor me.

"It was good to finish something I had left undone," she said. "It's made me happy." She bowed humbly to us. Then she got snooty again and waved us out.

"Well, you got to read to the end of it, didn't you, Akari?" I said as we walked home. Akari nodded, clutching the last pages of the story to her chest. I wanted to cry all over again. She looked so happy. Of course—the story had been written for her. For the first time, I thought it might be appropriate to thank Ms. Minakami. But Akari might still vanish because of her! I vowed never to let another word of thanks to her pass my lips.

"Do you want to go watch the fireworks tomorrow?" Yūsuke asked. It was late summer now, and there would be a fireworks display at the Naka River for Obon.

"Sounds good," I said. "See you tomorrow."

"Sounds good to me, too!" Akari answered.

The three of us went our separate ways.

~~~~

The next evening, Akari failed to appear at our meeting spot. When he saw me, Yūsuke yelled, "You're late! Let's go!" and started to set off.

"Shouldn't we wait for Akari?"

Yūsuke gave me a funny look. "Akari? Who are you talking about?"

"From our class! She lives behind me! Yesterday she promised to meet us."

"Kazu, the heat's gone to your head. Akari moved, remember?"

"She moved?" I said.

"Before summer vacation. She moved to Canada."

"What?!"

"Don't you remember? Some classmate you are!"

There was no point questioning him further.

"Uh, sorry. I can't go to the fireworks after all," I said. I sprinted to Akari's house.

The house was still there. Just like when I saw it the first time. It had no curtains. It stood vacant. A FOR RENT sign hung on the gate.

I zoomed to Minami Heights.

Ms. Minakami was gone. The super spotted me. "Ms. Minakami has moved away, young man," he said.

"What?!" I said for the second time that day. I couldn't believe my ears. Or my eyes.

"I was just here yesterday!" I told him. "She wasn't preparing to move at all!"

"Probably not," he replied. "She couldn't take much with her where she was going."

He told me she had moved to an assisted-living complex. "She took her valuables," he explained. "She asked us to sell the rest of her things."

I almost sank to the floor in a heap.

Where had Akari gone? Yūsuke said she'd left before summer. So maybe she hadn't vanished completely. I wanted to go see Ms. Minakami, but the super said she lived far away now. He knew the name of her town, but not her address.

With Akari and Ms. Minakami both gone, I spent the rest of the evening in a daze.

"Kazu, what's the matter with you? Do you have a crush on someone?" my sister asked, peering at my face. This was the third time she'd asked that tonight.

Around the time we heard the fireworks booming at the river, the phone rang.

"My goodness, hello! How is your new place? How is your mother?"

I figured the call was for Mom, but she yelled, "Kazu! For you! It's Akari!"

I seized the phone. "Akari! Is that really you? Are you OK?"

"I am, Kazu, I'm fine! I didn't disappear!" she replied. Her voice sounded distant.

"Are you really in Canada?" I asked.

"Yes. It was such a shock, Kazu! I woke up this morning, and here I was! And guess what? My mom is here, too, and all of our things. Everything we put together in Masuda— our furniture and dishes, even my swimsuit and yukata."

When Akari had come back to life, her house had been completely empty. But now her place was full of her possessions from Japan. That felt like proof somehow that she had lived here for a month in the summer, right when she first returned.

"Will you be all right over there, by yourself?" I asked.

I worried for her. To Akari, her own mother was still see-through.

"Yes, I'll be all right," she said. "I'm beginning to get used to this. And you helped me, Kazu, so I know I'll make it. I'm going to live! I know I can do it."

I said nothing. It felt like my words had all lodged in my chest.

"It looks like I'll live far away from Kimyō Temple Alley now, and start a new life totally separate from my old one," Akari went on. "I'll live in a place where no one knows I came back to life. In Masuda, I was practicing and getting ready for this. The vacation helped me prepare. Now, my new life can really begin!"

Akari sure was tough.

"Well, that's great," I said. "Now you can go to middle school and high school and university and fall in love and have a family."

"Right! And that family will not be invisible," she said. "I'm so excited, Kazu!"

I could imagine her clasping her hands to her chest and hopping, like always.

"But I won't forget, Kazu," she said. "I won't forget you, and so you can't forget me. Ever. I have 'The Moon Is on the Left' right here with me."

"I won't forget, don't worry," I said. "I'll remember you, and I'll remember the story."

"Good. That's a promise!"

The phone call ended. I stood there holding the receiver, dazed yet again.

Ms. Minakami had not burned the statuette. She had made me *think* she had, but she had kept it safe. Maybe she had been uncertain what to do. If the statuette were lost, it would affect not only the returned spirits but also their families and offspring. She had said that to me, right?

If she'd been so uncertain, she could have told me! Then I would never have had to hate her or worry about Akari vanishing. I couldn't believe that stubborn granny. Oh, well. The important thing was, Akari would live.

Akari was going to live!

Summer vacation ended. The stifling heat began to seem like a dream as cool breezes blew. I thought of Akari and wondered how she was.

I couldn't forget her or Kimyō Temple, or "The Moon Is on the Left." I could never forget because . . . Kiriko came to live with us. Kiriko with her big wide face, acting like our place had always been hers.

"Kazu! Kazu!" my mom shouted. "Come in here, will you? Kiri-chan killed a mouse!"

I'd been demoted from eldest son to catsitter. Kiriko saw this as a promotion for me, no doubt. Naturally our old house harbored mice. She enjoyed recreational hunting like royalty.

The night of the fireworks show, the super from Minami Heights had run to our place with a pale face. He carried Kiriko together with her special cushion, her food, and even her kitty litter. He had just realized she was still in Minami Heights. A note had been left with her.

The note said that Kiriko had been promised to me, so would I please take care of her.

I moaned aloud. *Seriously?* Ms. Minakami had said there was a favor she wanted instead of a shoulder massage— but I hadn't expected this!

Mom wore a sour face about it, but Dad helped by saying that one cat would hardly be noticed in our large house. My sister bonded with Kiriko instantly. Those two were just alike: they both drove me nuts.

Soon after school started, Ms. Minakami sent me a letter.

Kazu-kun,

You must be mad because I left without saying anything. Or maybe you're glad to be rid of me?

At any rate, I couldn't burn the statuette. I made you think I did, but from the day I stole it I never could figure out what to do with it. I still don't think there should be a Kimyō Temple. The whole idea may just be myth. But if there really were people who returned to life, some of them might have had families. There could be scores of Polonia, in other words. I didn't know what would happen to those people—so I chose not to burn it.

I never took Kimyō Temple seriously before this summer. I thought it was legend. But Kazu-kun, you believed. You were desperate. You were frantically trying to save someone all by yourself, and you were quite a brave young man. Seeing your determination, I thought you were right, and I changed.

When you and Akari-chan came to my apartment, I saw that she might be a ghost. You said only that she was a classmate, without telling me where she lived. You didn't want me to know she was your neighbor, did you? You looked so guilty after that! You might as well have come out and told me she was a child of Kimyō Temple! Plus _Daisy_ is such an old magazine! I could hardly help thinking it had something to do with a returned ghost. And _Daisy_ is a magazine for girls.

So, Akari is a returned spirit, is she? Kazu-kun, you brought her to me because you thought I had burned the statuette, but what you did was dangerous. I might have blurted out "Child of Kimyō Temple" right then and there!

Then again, I never could have. You, Kazu, were working so hard to protect Akari. And she was lovely. For the first time I believed that the myth might be more than just a story. It made me glad that I had not burned the statuette in the first place. I'm not some horrible demon, you know.

Anyway, I decided that, like you and your family, there was nothing for me to do but keep silent about the spirits who have returned and protect them. It made me angry because it felt like I'd lost to you. But now I think that was a good thing.

Thank you for making me finish "The Moon Is on the Left." I had given up on that dream and buried my disappointment for years, but finishing that project made the hopes of my youth come flooding back. When I completed the tale, I felt that perhaps I could die now with no regrets. But not so fast. I have no intention of *dying soon, as you well know. And I do not wish to have further regrets. I'm stubborn that way.*

I left the statuette with someone trustworthy. I don't know if more spirits will return. You must think it would be fine if they did. Kiriko likes that about you. So do I.

Respectfully yours,

Sato Minakami

P.S. Finishing "The Moon Is on the Left" was such fun, I plan to write another tale. I'm going to enter it in a Debut Novelist contest. Be sure to celebrate when my first book comes out!

Oh, boy.

ABOUT THE AUTHOR

SACHIKO KASHIWABA is a prolific writer of children's and young adult fantasy whose career spans more than four decades. Her works have garnered the prestigious Sankei, Shogakukan, and Noma children's literature awards, and her novel *The Marvelous Village Veiled in Mist* influenced Hayao Miyazaki's film *Spirited Away*. Her books for children include the Monster Hotel series, *Ōobasan no fushigi na reshipi* (Great-aunt's amazing recipes), *Mirakuru famirī* (Miracle family), *Tsuzuki no toshokan* (The what's-next library), *Temple Alley Summer*, *Ōsama ni koi shita majo* (The witch who loved the king), and *Chikashitsu kara no fushigi na tabi* (Strange journey from the basement), lately animated as *The Wonderland*. She has co-translated two fairy novels by Gail Carson Levine into Japanese, and she edited a children's version of the *Tōno monogatari*, beloved folk legends collected by Kizen Sasaki and Kunio Yanagita. She lives in Iwate Prefecture, Japan.

ABOUT THE ILLUSTRATOR

MIHO SATAKE is a Japanese artist and illustrator. She is best known for illustrating the Japanese editions of several classic children's books including *Howl's Moving Castle* by Diana Wynne Jones, three books in the *Kiki's Delivery Service* series by Eiko Kadono, and the twentieth-anniversary edition of the *Harry Potter* series.

ABOUT THE TRANSLATOR

AVERY FISCHER UDAGAWA grew up in Kansas and studied English and Asian studies at St. Olaf College in Minnesota. She holds an MA in advanced Japanese studies from the University of Sheffield. She has studied at Nanzan University, Nagoya, on a Fulbright fellowship, and at the Inter-University Center for Japanese Language Studies, Yokohama. She writes, translates, and works in international education near Bangkok, where she lives with her bicultural family.

YONDER is an imprint from Restless Books devoted to bringing the wealth of great stories from around the globe to English-reading children, middle graders, and young adults. Books from other countries, cultures, viewpoints, and storytelling traditions can open up a universe of possibility, and the wider our view, the more powerfully books enrich and expand us. In an increasingly complex, globalized world, stories are potent vehicles of empathy. We believe it is essential to teach our kids to place themselves in the shoes of others beyond their communities, and instill in them a lifelong curiosity about the world and their place in it. Through publishing a diverse array of transporting stories, Yonder nurtures the next generation of savvy global citizens and lifelong readers.

Visit us at restlessbooks.org/yonder